The Ghost at Mahone Bay

The Ghost at Mahone Bay
An Angela and Emmie Adventure

Tom Schwarzkopf

NIMBUS
PUBLISHING

Copyright © Tom Schwarzkopf 2005

Nimbus Publishing Limited
PO Box 9166
Halifax, NS   B3K 5M8
(902) 455-4286

Printed and bound in Canada
Cover illustration: J. O. Pennanen
Interior Design: Margaret Issenman, MGDC

Library and Archives Canada Cataloguing in Publication

Schwarzkopf, Tom, 1943-
The ghost at Mahone Bay / Tom Schwarzkopf.
ISBN 1-55109-526-2
I. Title.

PS8637.C594G46 2005   jC813'.6   C2005-901990-5

We acknowledge the financial support of the Government of Canada through the Book Publishing Industry Development Program (BPIDP) and the Canada Council, and of the Province of Nova Scotia through the Department of Tourism, Culture and Heritage for our publishing activities.

Acknowledgements

Even though writing is a lonely activity, no book happens without the support and encouragement of many friends.

This book was written for Angela, who asked for a new chapter to the adventure each night. Thank you for loving it.

My family, especially my life-long friend and partner, Jane, have encouraged me at every step. Thanks for your faith in my creativity.

Thanks to my in-laws for happy times in Angela's house, and Gram, thank you for the ghost stories.

For the kind, caring attention I received from the many wonderful people at Nimbus, I am very grateful, and pleased that you became so fond of the two girls.

Contents

CHAPTER 1

Summer Holidays

"Ten whole weeks of freedom!" Emmie Seegal threw herself down on the grass next to her best friend, Angela Black. "Two and a half months, seventy days, and zillions of minutes of nothing to do but enjoy summer." She propped herself up on her elbows and looked intently at Angela, who was deep into her book. For a moment Emmie just lay there, her mass of red curls bouncing lightly in the breeze blowing across the lawn, a big grin on her freckled face. "School is over," she said, "and a whole summer of adventure lies ahead."

Angela finished her page and looked up. *What a contrast to last summer,* she thought. A year ago this week she had been uprooted and moved from her home in Ottawa to the quiet seaside town of Mahone Bay, Nova Scotia. Her father had announced that they were moving thousands of miles from her lifelong friends to the outskirts of this small East Coast tourist town, and she was sure then that her whole life had been ruined. Her brother, Matthew, took it easier, but he was going to go back to Ottawa in the fall for his second year of college, while she was faced with a strange new school and the difficulty of trying to make new friends. What a terrible summer it would have been, if she hadn't met Emmie.

Emmie lived on the farm that bordered the back of Angela's place, high on the hill above a wooded area that Angela called the Enchanted Forest. Once an old path up the hill had been rediscovered and re-cleared, the girls were able to visit frequently and had become best friends. When school started, they entered grade six together, and Emmie introduced Angela to her school friends, most of whom lived in the town. Emmie and Angela were two of the very few living outside the village, so they spent most of their spare time together.

It didn't hurt, either, that both girls liked the same things—listening to music, taking walks along the seashore at low tide, and reading books from the library where Angela's mom worked part time. And, much to Angela's surprise, there was a lot to keep two girls busy and entertained in this little seaside town.

Now the school term was over, and they lay contemplating their freedom on Angela's front lawn, which gently sloped down to the road and the seashore beyond. Above them, Angela's big, white house sat on a flat area halfway up the hill. Just visible through the trees was the yellow clapboard of Emmie's farmhouse crowning the hill, surrounded by old oaks, chestnuts and maple trees.

Angela would have been content to spend the summer reading in the shade of the old oak on her front lawn, but Emmie clearly had other ideas.

"I had a brilliant thought this morning," she announced.

Angela groaned. "Your brilliant thoughts usually get us into trouble. Like when you said there was buried treasure behind my house, but when we dug, we broke that water pipe and washed out the whole side of the hill, for instance." She shut the book and sat up. "All right, what is it?" she said, expecting the worst.

"My mom's working late every day now at the café, cooking for all the tourists, so someone needs to mind the house. And it gets way too quiet when there's just me and the cat. So I thought we could have the world's longest sleepover up on my farm,"

Emmie said triumphantly, "and we'll sleep in my room all summer, and take care of the chickens and the garden, and—"

"I don't know," said Angela, picking at the tiny blue wildflowers that grew everywhere in the grass.

"What? Why?"

"It's, well, it's just that your house is kind of…"

"Creepy?"

"Well…yeah. It's just so old."

"So's yours!"

Angela turned and pointed to the date cast in the concrete bottom step of her porch—1919. "It's not really that old," she said. "Your house goes back to the eighteen hundreds."

"Lots of places are that old in Mahone Bay, and you don't think they're creepy." Emmie looked over at the book Angela was reading. She had a sudden thought.

"What're you reading? I bet it's something spooky and it's got you freaked out!"

"It's nothing exciting." Angela tried to cover the book with her hand, but Emmie grabbed it—*Nova Scotia Ghosts.*

"It's all about ghosts that haunt this province." Angela said, trying to defend her reading choice.

"Well, you're spooking yourself out for nothing, you know, 'cause there's no such thing."

"As what?"

"As ghosts," Emmie declared.

"There is, otherwise they wouldn't have written this book."

"Those are just stories." Emmie stood up and tossed her head, the better to assert her authority. "I'll bet it's kept in the fiction section of the library."

Angela turned the book over and read the label on the spine. "'Mahone Bay Public Library—Non-Fiction.' So there!"

Emmie paused. "So you don't want to stay at my house because you're scared there's a ghost?"

"No! I'm not scared." Angela got up and turned so Emmie couldn't see her red face.

"Well, my mom says there's no such thing as ghosts, and she's been living here all her life."

"Okay, fine," Angela said, in what she hoped was a confident voice.

"'Okay'?" Emmie asked. "So our sleepover is on?"

"All right." Angela tried to sound interested as she turned and started toward her house, still clutching her ghost book. "Let's go ask my mom if I can stay at your place."

CHAPTER 2

Sleepover

"Well," said Mrs. Black, "if you two can stand each other for that long, and Emmie's mom doesn't mind, I don't see a problem. You'll be good company for each other when I'm working at the library. I'm sure, Emmie, that it gets quite lonely up there rattling around in that big old farm house, with your dad at sea and your mom working."

At the word "lonely," Angela shivered.

Her mother didn't notice. "And if you two have any trouble, you can always call me or just run down the hill."

Emmie was sure Angela's mom was referring to the two girls' amazing ability to get into difficulties without even trying, and then having to be rescued by their parents.

"There won't be any problems, I promise," Emmie said, putting on a solemn face.

"I'm sure there won't be, but I'll just check with your mother," Mrs. Black replied, picking up the phone and dialing. "Hello, Margaret, this is Jane. These girls have just proposed an interesting idea…"

Angela and Emmie ran upstairs to get ready.

A short time later, the girls were struggling up the steep path to Emmie's house, carrying Angela's sleeping bag and her overnighter full of clothes and books. Soon they were at the door of the old farmhouse. Although it was well over a hundred years old, most of it had been renovated and was quite modern. They passed through the large farm kitchen, with its enormous wood-burning stove and smaller electric one. Since Emmie's mother was one of the cooks at the Point Café, she often prepared pies or soups on the big stove and then took them in with her to town.

They passed through the large living room, which had a wall of windows looking down the hill to the sea. Upstairs, the master bedroom was at one end of the hall, next to the top of the staircase, but Emmie's room was all the way at the other end of the hall, directly across from her father's study. At the end of the hall, right beside Emmie's room, was a door to the attic stairs, always kept tightly shut because Emmie's mom was deathly afraid of mice getting downstairs from the attic. Angela walked past the door quickly, trying not to be creeped out by this old part of the farmhouse. Emmie's room, at least, was sunny and cheerful and new-looking, with bright blue walls covered with posters and photographs, and a thick, yellow carpet on the floor.

Angela unpacked her sleeping bag, spread it out on the floor, and opened her overnight bag. She dug out her book and sprawled out on the sleeping bag to read while Emmie flipped through a comic.

"Still reading ghost stories?" Emmie asked after a few minutes. "Come on, you don't believe in that stuff, do you?"

Angela sighed and sat up. "I really don't know. I mean, these are supposed to be based on people seeing actual ghosts, but I'm not sure I believe it. Then again, I'm not sure they don't exist. Maybe if I saw one I'd believe." She laughed nervously.

"Well, my mom's seen a lot, and if she says they don't exist, then that's good enough for me," Emmie said. She stopped as she heard something outside on the gravel drive.

"Hey, do you hear a car?" She looked out the

window. "It's Mom. Let's go down and see if she wants help with dinner."

"Mom, have you seen Bootsie lately?" Emmie put the last of the dinner dishes on the kitchen counter.

"No, I haven't, dear, but you know what that cat is like, such an independent one." Mrs. Seegal turned off the tap, added soap to the steaming sink full of dishes, and began to wash them, placing them on the rack at the side of the sink to drain.

Emmie grabbed two dishtowels and handed one to Angela. "Well, it's just that I haven't seen her for days, and she hasn't touched her dry food or come in for any canned food."

"I wouldn't worry. She's a bit like a barn cat, able to take care of herself, but she won't roam too far and she never goes down near the highway. She's probably chasing mice in the fields and has a full tummy."

"Well, maybe." Emmie polished a glass and set it down on the counter. "She has been getting pretty tubby lately."

After the girls finished drying the dishes, they went back up to Emmie's bedroom, agreeing that they were too tired and full to do anything but read. Every so often Angela would read Emmie a particularly juicy or spooky part of a ghost story, trying to convince her that the stories could be real, but Emmie would try to ignore her by quoting solid facts from her book on unusual animals.

At ten o'clock Emmie's mother came up to the bedroom. "Okay, you bookworms, it's time to brush your teeth. And lights out in half an hour."

In the bathroom, Angela took advantage of Emmie's mouthful of toothpaste.

"You didn't even hear the story about Charlotte MacCormack. She was locked up in her root cellar for five weeks and died, and now whenever anyone goes in there—"

Emmie spat into the sink. "I can't believe you read that stuff! *I* could make up better ghost stories."

Even after the lights were out, the debate continued, Angela full of new ghost stories and Emmie too practical to believe them. Finally, tired and running out of arguments, Emmie announced she was going to sleep and rolled over. Soon she was breathing softly and steadily.

Angela lay awake for a long time, listening to

her best friend sleeping. The old farmhouse creaked and cracked as the building cooled off in the night air and settled. A full moon spilled its silver light through the open window and a ghostly breeze moved the curtains ever so slightly. Somewhere in the Enchanted Forest, an owl hooted before setting out for his nightly hunt.

Gradually, though, Angela's eyes got heavy, and she drifted off into an uneasy sleep.

CHAPTER 3

Ghostly Happenings

Thump.

Angela opened her eyes. It was the middle of the night, and the moonlight fell from a different angle through the window. *What was that noise?* she wondered. *Maybe Emmie fell out of her bed again.* It had been a running joke at school to ask Emmie each morning where she had slept the night before. More often than not, she had rolled out of bed in her sleep and spent the night on the floor, wrapped in her blankets.

Angela looked across the room. The red curls spilling over the pillow on Emmie's bed told her that, for once, Emmie was still on top of it.

Thump. There it was again, and it seemed to be coming from up above. Angela was wide awake now.

Thump...scrape. There was a pause, then another thump. Angela sat up in her sleeping bag. The sounds had definitely come from the attic—more precisely, from the attic stairs on the other side of the wall behind Emmie's bed.

Scrrrrrape...thump. Angela felt the hair on the back of her neck getting prickly. Her mind flashed unwillingly through all the ghost stories she had been reading, but she couldn't remember any having to do with ghostly noises and the Mahone Bay area.

THUMP! Angela jumped to her feet. This time it was even loud enough to stir Emmie, who rolled over and slowly opened her eyes. She looked at Angela, standing in the moonlight, sleeping bag around her ankles, her pale face framed by long tangles of dark hair.

"What was that?" Emmie asked sleepily.

"I—I don't know," Angela managed to whisper, "but I think it's coming from the attic stairs."

Emmie sat up and listened, but there was nothing but silence. After a few moments she lay back down. "Your imagination is working overtime, Angela." She started to roll over. "Too many ghost stories on the brain—"

THUMP! They both jumped. Emmie sat bolt upright. The two girls strained to listen. There was a long silence, then a scraping sound, as if something was dragging across a stair. Then there was a pause, then another *THUMP*. Emmie grabbed a flashlight from beside her bed and swung her feet to the floor. They both crept quietly to the doorway of her room.

Except for the faint glow from the night light in the bathroom, the hall was quiet, dark and deserted. The other bedroom door, down the hall, was shut, and so was the attic door beside them .

"Do…do you…think it's…" Angela paused. "Do you think it's a ghost?" She was whispering, both out of fear and in an attempt to not wake Emmie's mother.

"Of course not!" Emmie whispered back.

They were standing in the hall now, facing the dark wooden attic door with its tarnished brass doorknob. It was the only original door still in the old farmhouse; the Seegals had never bothered to replace it. Now it seemed to stare at the two girls in their nightgowns, as if hiding a dark secret.

"Then what was that?" Angela's voice quivered. "Was it just the house settling?"

"I don't think so. Mice, maybe?" Emmie was trying very hard to look practical.

"A mouse couldn't make that big a noise."

"Okay, then a rat." Emmie was getting less and less sure of herself. "Anyway, it's gone—"

THUMP. This time it was so loud that they both jumped, the flashlight falling from Emmie's hand and rolling along the hall carpet. At that very moment, a breeze blew through Emmie's bedroom window, which they could still see through the doorway, and the curtains rustled. Then the attic door creaked open a crack.

Angela and Emmie stood rooted in fear on the hall carpet. Angela felt every bit of energy drain from her body. She couldn't speak or move. Emmie also seemed to be frozen. The flashlight lay on the floor, its beam uselessly lighting up a patch of carpet.

A strong gust blew the curtains wide into the bedroom, and the old attic door swung noiselessly open.

The setting moon was still high enough to spill some of its eerie, blue light through a small, grimy, cobweb-covered window high up in the attic. It was just visible over the top of the attic stairs, but it wasn't bright enough to cast any light down the staircase. Angela thought that she saw a misty shape flicker through the moonlight.

Then something moved in the darkness.

SCRRRRRRRAPE!

Both girls were absolutely terrified. Angela felt as if she was trapped in a block of ice. She struggled to speak, but her tongue was dried out and stuck fast to the inside of her mouth, which was frozen shut with fear. Her arms were like lead, and all her hair, even the fuzz on her arms, felt like porcupine quills. The seconds crawled by like hours. The tick-tock of the grandfather clock downstairs seemed to sound in slow motion.

Angela struggled to speak again. With a tremendous effort she opened her mouth and uttered in a croaky, shaky voice a command that popped into her head from one of the ghost stories.

"Sp-sp-speak, spirit, or b-b-be gone."

The clock ticked slowly in the parlour below. The moon illuminated the spiderwebs over the window. A cold mist seemed to settle over everything in the hall.

Then, after an eternity, something spoke.

CHAPTER 4

Spirits Revealed

Mew!

Angela and Emmie looked at each other—*mew?* Suddenly all the fear washed away. Emmie bent down, picked up the flashlight and aimed it at the ghost.

There in the yellow beam of the flashlight, sprawled on the stair, was a tiny white kitten with black ears, a black nose and a long, skinny, black-tipped tail.

Mew, said the kitten plaintively, as it tried to stand on its wobbly legs.

"What the heck is going on here, girls?" They turned to find Emmie's mother standing in the hall in her nightgown looking very sleepy and very displeased.

"There was this thumping noise—"

"I was sure it was a ghost—"

"—scraping across the stairs—"

"—so I got up to check—"

"Stop! One girl at a time," said Mrs. Seegal grumpily. "Now what happened? Oh my, what a tiny kitten." She pushed between the girls and bent down to pick it up. "My goodness, this fellow must be just a week or so old. See, his eyes are just about open. Now, how on earth did you get down these stairs, little guy? Where did you come from?"

"BOOTSIE!" Angela and Emmie shouted at once and leapt up the attic stairs, barely pausing to turn on the light switch as they raced by.

"Over here," Emmie called after a minute of searching. "She's got her kittens in an old box of magazines, here in the corner behind the spinning wheel."

Angela rushed over, followed closely by Emmie's mother, still holding the runaway kitten. Bootsie lay listlessly in the box with two more balls of fluff curled up next to her. She raised her head weakly when she saw Emmie and tried to meow.

"Oh no," said Emmie, "she's been locked up here for days without any food or water. Mom, she's dying!"

"I don't think she's dying, what with the mice up here to catch," said Emmie's mother as she knelt beside the box and returned the wayward kitten to its mother, "but I think we'd better get her and her family down to the kitchen and get some real food and water into her pronto."

The procession wound its way down the attic stairs, through the hall and down to the kitchen, Emmie's mom carrying the box and Emmie and Angela trailing behind. Emmie dished out some cat food and Angela filled Bootsie's water dish as Emmie's mom settled the box beside the wood stove. Bootsie slowly rose and wobbled her way out of the box and over to the food, where she ate steadily for several minutes before drinking deeply and returning to the kittens. Then she settled down, stretched out, and allowed them to nurse. She purred gently as they slurped away, and Angela thought she looked happier already.

"Now where do you suppose she got pregnant?" Emmie asked.

"Good grief," said her mother, "there's enough cats passing by this area. Some of them come from other farms, and some are semi-wild, like our barn cats—they come and go as they please, and eat what they can find. I often see strange cats sneaking food out of the barn cats' dishes."

"Three kittens! Oh, it's so exciting," said Emmie.

"Three kittens to find a home for. Not so exciting," countered her tired mother.

"Oh, but Mom, they're so cute! Look—one is all grey, she's such a cutie. I think I'll call her that: 'Cutie.'"

"And the white-and-black one we'll call Spook, because he spooked us on the stairs," added Angela.

"And what about the brown-and-black one?"

"That's quite enough for one night," interrupted Emmie's mother. "I have to get an early start in the morning. There are three busloads coming to the café for lunch; that's thirty-five people times three, in only two hours—plus whatever walks in the door. So I've got a heap of cooking to start in the morning. And with Emmie's father away," she said firmly, looking at the girls standing there in their nightdresses, "I will need help! There's onions to be chopped and potatoes to be peeled and clams to be shucked."

"Yes, Mom."

"Yes, Mrs. Seegal."

"Now off to bed with you. Bootsie will be fine here. And close that attic door properly, Emily Louise!"

"Emily Louise?" Angela whispered a giggle as they raced up the stairs.

"Mom only calls me that when she's either very serious or very mad. It's what my Gram calls me too, but I never use my middle name." She tossed her red curls defiantly, and firmly shut the attic door.

"Why not? I think 'Emmie Lou' would be nice." The two girls were snuggled back into bed by now and they could hear Mrs. Seegal's door close.

"I don't know. I just don't like it. What about you, Angela MARIE?"

"Okay. Point taken."

"Now we'll have to find homes for the kittens," sighed Emmie. "Oh well, at least they can stay here until they're old enough to be adopted." She thought for a moment, then giggled. "Well, that was an interesting ghost of yours, Miss Angela."

"It sure sounded like one to me," Angela replied in a small voice as she snuggled deeper into the sleeping bag.

The moon was down now, the room deep in darkness. Both girls were silent. After a few minutes, Emmie rolled over and drifted easily off to sleep. Angela lay awake on her back, looking up at the glowing stick-on stars on Emmie's ceiling. Just how *did* that little kitten get all the way across the attic and down those stairs when it could barely stand on its wobbly legs? And what was it that she had seen when the attic door swung open—that flickering shape? Was it her imagination? Or was it...

The next thing she knew, the sun was streaming through the window and Emmie's mom was banging pots around in the kitchen below.

CHAPTER 5

Kitten Mischief

"Mom, do you think Gram would like a kitten?"

Emmie's mother stopped rolling the immense slab of pie dough that covered the kitchen counter, and thought for a moment. She was making a batch of strawberry pies for the café while Angela and Emmie played with the kittens in the corner. She dusted the dough with more flour and continued rolling.

"I really don't know, dear. She does live alone in that flat, with only Mrs. Potter downstairs."

"I mean, she had a cat before, and I thought maybe she'd like a companion kitten." Emmie was getting worried now that the kittens were growing so quickly. It had been three weeks since they found Spook on the attic stair, and now that the kittens were weaned, they were all over the kitchen most days. The two girls' job today was to keep the kittens from being stepped on while Emmie's mother baked.

"Well, you could always drop over and ask her, dear. I feel guilty about not getting over more, but it's been so busy this season. I could take you girls with me at noon when I go to the café, and you could poke around town and then visit Gram."

Angela scooped up the smallest kitten, the brown-and-black one that still didn't have a name. He was the rascally one, always getting into some sort of trouble. For the littlest, he was quite a handful.

"I asked my parents if I could have Spook, and they didn't say no." Angela tried to sound hopeful. It was true her parents hadn't said no, but they hadn't said yes, either.

"Well, you could take her down the hill for your mother to see after I get the pies in the oven, and I'll watch the other two until you get back."

Soon the two friends were walking through Angela's back door, Emmie carrying their precious cargo. Angela's mother melted when she saw the little white kitten with his delicate black highlights. She tried, of course, to be sensible about having a pet, but Angela could see she was smitten.

"Now, Angela," she said, "you realize someone will have to feed it and change the litter and make sure it doesn't go too far, and that someone won't be me. Understand?"

"Yes, Mother, I promise I will come down each day and take the best care of Spook and feed him every day." Angela tried to answer her mother in her most serious voice.

"And change the litter?"

"And change the litter." This was said with somewhat less enthusiasm.

Some time later, the two girls went back up the hill with their arms empty, and Angela's mother was left to play with the new kitten.

Later that day they arrived at Emmie's grandmother's home. She lived on the second floor of an old house in the middle of Mahone Bay. She owned the whole house, but it was too much house for one person, so she had turned the upstairs into a self-contained flat with a kitchen, bathroom, sitting room, and bedroom. She rented out the downstairs to another elderly woman, and sometimes they walked together or played rummy. Grandma Wilder lived a pretty independent life for someone who almost eighty years old. She would sit on her balcony with her knitting and look out over the town's government wharf, watching the comings and goings of sailboats and motorboats all day. Her late husband had been a mate on a sailing schooner, and she never tired of watching the daily activity of a seaside town.

Emmie and Angela rang the doorbell and let themselves into the hall. They climbed the dark wooden stairs with its turned railings and knocked on Gram's door.

A few minutes later, the two young ladies, as Gram always called them, were seated in big wicker armchairs on the balcony with frosty glasses of iced tea in hand. They brought Gram up to speed on all the family happenings, especially Bootsie's kittens.

"Gram," Emmie eventually said, with a coy grin, "I think that you need a companion to keep you company."

Gram looked at her, and Angela could tell that Gram knew exactly what was coming. "And who would want to live with me, Emily Louise?"

Emmie ignored the formal name and continued. "You haven't had a cat since Patch went, and this one's so cute and quiet and it needs someone to love it, and I'm sure it wouldn't be a problem and—"

"Oh dear child, slow down or your lips will fall off." She paused to reflect. "Well…" Both girls leaned forward in their seats. "Well, it has been quiet around here with Patch gone now for, let me see…" She was agonizingly slow when she wanted to be. "It must be two years now. Hmm, a kitten, eh? Well, I'll have to see it, and talk to your mother. You see, the only problem is that someone," and she looked straight at Emmie, "will have to come into town every day when I take my midwinter trip with the girls to Arizona, and feed the kitten and change the litter."

"Oh, I promise I'll come in and feed Cutie."

"Is that its name?"

"Yes, but you can change it if you want."

"Did I hear you say you'd change the litter?" said Gram. At this Angela snickered.

"Yes, Gram," answered Emmie, shooting Angela a dark look.

It was a warm summer day with a gentle breeze off the water as the two girls walked through town, passing Old Painter Art Supplies and the Pots and Pans Shoppe and, around the corner, the Wool and Knits Barn and the Point Café. They climbed the hill that led away from town, keeping carefully to the side of the road, and an hour later arrived at Emmie's, hot and dusty. Emmie's mother had shut the kittens into the downstairs bathroom, and they were all too willing to run as soon as the door was opened.

After being chased and captured, the squirming kittens were cuddled in the girls' arms and finally settled down. At least, Cutie was settled. The brown-and-black one had other ideas and dug his tiny needle claws into Angela's arm, then launched himself out of her arms and scooted under the wood stove. He was too far back to catch and too clever to come out where the girls could grab him.

"He's such a little rascal!" said Angela, nursing the pin pricks on her arm left by his claws.

"He's always escaping and getting into places where he shouldn't be," answered Emmie from the floor by the stove. "Oh, he fell asleep under there! The devil! Now we'll never get him out."

"What should we call him?" pondered Angela. "We can't go around calling 'Hey You,' can we?"

"I vote for Devil," said Emmie, straightening up.

"No, that's too mean. He's not evil, he's just rebellious…what about Rascal?"

So the rascally little kitten had a name.

"EMILY LOUISE!!!"

The girls jumped. They were in Emmie's room, and Emmie's mother was rolling pie crusts in the kitchen below—exactly where this cry of anguish and anger was coming from.

"Emily, you get down here this instant!"

Angela and Emmie tumbled down the stairs and into the kitchen. Emmie's mother stood there, her flour-covered hands clutching a rolling pin and her face as red as the strawberries that covered the table. The long counter was covered with rolled-out dough spotted with tiny sooty footprints. Rascal was sprawled out in the middle of a patch of fresh pie crust, dusty with cobwebs and soot, his tummy bulging with the dough he had eaten. He had dropped for a nap right beside the gaping hole in the pastry dough, and Emmie's mother was trying to get him off the counter.

"Emmie, that cat has got to go."

"But he's just a baby!"

"He's more than I can cope with. He's trouble!"

"But Rascal's so small."

"'Rascal'? Well, that just about says it all. No arguments, Emily. I can't work with that kitten always underfoot, and now this." She waved the rolling pin at Rascal as Emmie scooped up the flour-covered kitten.

"I'm sorry, Emmie, but this sets me back at least half an hour, and I'm already pushing it to get the pies down to the café in time for supper. You have to find him a home, pronto."

The girls rushed Rascal upstairs, ran a bath, and, with the kitten protesting with his voice, teeth and claws, scrubbed him and wrapped him in an old towel.

"Oh, Rascal, you little rascal. Getting into the pies," said Angela, scolding the kitten in a mock serious voice. Then, remembering the sight of him in the middle of the pastry dough, the girls collapsed into fits of giggles. Fearing that Mrs. Seegal would hear them, they crept off to Emmie's bedroom with the bundled kitten, shut the door, and burst out laughing again.

After a minute, Emmie turned serious. "What'll we do now? I so wanted to keep him, he's so small."

"My mom says that if kittens have big paws, they'll grow up to be big cats," consoled Angela. "Look at his paws—they're huge compared to the rest of him. Somehow I don't think he'll be a runt forever. Anyway, from what I know of your mom, if she says Rascal's gotta go, we'd better find him a home quick."

"I guess," Emmie sighed. "But Bootsie's kittens are too good for just any home. What are we going to do with him?" She was silent for a long time. "I've got it," she announced finally. "We'll run an ad in the paper."

CHAPTER 6

The Adoption Agency

"Well this is quite interesting." Mr. Woodward took off his reading glasses and laid them on the counter. "And so well-written, too. At least two of my students have been able to stay awake in my classes," he chuckled.

Mr. Woodward, in addition to being the editor of the local newspaper, *Time 'n Tide*, was their English teacher in school. Or perhaps it was the other way around. In any case, he had his editor's hat on now that school was out, and was reading the advertisement that Angela and Emmie had crafted.

"Very ingenious to make it like an adoption. And clever to want to interview possible owners of this kitten." He smiled at them.

"Oh, we're serious about the interview," explained Emmie. "We want to make sure that Rascal will go to a home where he'll be well taken care of, and loved and spoiled."

"Well, I'm sure he will. Rascal, eh? That's quite the name."

"He earned it," said Angela. "He's always getting into trouble, even though he's the runt of the litter."

"Will the ad run in this week's paper?" Emmie looked worried.

"Let me see what it looks like. Have you ever seen the layout program on my computer?"

Mr. Woodward led them over to the computer desk that sat in the front sunroom of his house, which served as the newspaper office. He had started the paper six years ago when he came to Mahone Bay to teach, and fell in love with the town and its people. During the school year he published the paper weekly, writing most of it, laying it out on his computer and taking it over to Bridgewater to be printed. It was distributed by school children, who were paid five cents a copy to deliver it, and everyone in Mahone Bay got a copy free—advertising paid the costs of producing it. In the summer, when the tourists were in town, he published twice a week and made it available for seventy-five cents at local stores.

He showed the girls the pages of the next issue and pointed to a blank space on one page. "Now, your little ad will just fit in the space I couldn't fill.

So I'll give you a reduced rate—say, five dollars?"

With the money they had left over, the girls headed for the lunch counter at William's General Store and got large ice cream cones. Eleanor, the server, dished up their favourites without them even having to ask—she was so used to her regular customers. Eleanor knew everyone in Mahone Bay, all their families, where they came from, and anything else you would care to know. But she didn't think of herself as a gossip, exactly. As she always said, "I only tell what any soul would tell you if they were here, and nothin' else I hear passes my lips."

Ice creams finished, Emmie and Angela took the long walk back to Emmie's house and waited for the paper to come out in two days' time.

"Emmie, there's a gentleman on the phone for you. I think it's about your advertisement." Mrs. Seegal handed the phone to Emmie as Angela hovered close by.

"Yup. Yup, of course. Yes, that sounds all right. Just a minute, I'll ask my mother." Emmie covered the phone. "His name is Angus Targus and he lives alone on Mason's Island. He wants a cat for company. Can he come by tomorrow and meet Rascal?"

Emmie's mother nodded.

"About two," continued Emmie into the phone, "Yup, that's fine. Do you know where we live? Oh yeah, Alister knows us well. Okay. Thanks. Bye."

"Well?" said Angela as Emmie hung up, "Tell me, tell me!" She was dancing with excitement.

"Let me see. He knows Alister. They talk by radio a lot, since he doesn't have a phone on the island."

Alister was the town handyman, grass cutter, and snow shoveller for those who couldn't take care of such things by themselves, and he was one of the most beloved of Mahone Bay's inhabitants. He was the kind of person who wouldn't think twice about getting up at three in the morning to come over and restart your furnace, and he often ran errands for the elderly but wouldn't take a cent for it. He was also an expert amateur radio operator.

Emmie continued: "Actually, I remember Alister telling me about him—he's a retired ferryboat captain and he moved to the island with his wife, but she died last year, so now he lives alone."

"Well, if he's friends with Alister, that's a recommendation for sure," said Emmie's mother. "Now that you've described him, I think I know who Captain Targus is. Now, girls, I'd like the place tidied up for tomorrow, please. He's coming at two?"

"Yup. He said he'll be coming to town by boat, and he'll borrow Alister's car to get up here. We'll make sure the place is clean by then, I promise."

The girls went outside, Angela eager for more information. "Well? Do you think he's a good candidate?"

"I think so; he didn't make fun of us for wanting to interview Rascal's possible owner. He said it was very responsible of us to screen adopters."

As they talked, Bootsie stalked past them, her head and tail in the air and her trademark black paws padding in the dirt. She turned away from Emmie and walked stiffly over to the barn, where she disappeared into its gloomy shadows.

"She's mad at me for taking away her kittens, you know. But Gram is so happy with Cutie."

"My mom hardly gives me any chance to visit Spook, she's hogging him all the time," said Angela.

They strolled down the hill along the path that joined their houses. As they neared Angela's house, they could see her father getting into his car.

"I bet he's going to town!" said Angela. "Dad, wait!"

They ran the last hundred yards and threw themselves, panting, into the car.

"We can ask Eleanor more about the Captain," Angela said to Emmie once they caught their breath, "and since we'll be at Williams', we can have a little snack…"

Soon they found themselves once again on the chrome and red-leather stools of William's lunch counter, spooning up ice cream and talking to Eleanor.

CHAPTER 7

Rascal and the Captain

Mrs. Seegal ushered Captain Angus Targus into the living room the following afternoon, and was offering him a cup of tea when the girls came noisily downstairs. The Captain was a handsome, slightly built, older gentleman, dressed in a white golf shirt and a blue jacket that was undone. He had salt-and-pepper, close-cropped hair and a beard to match, and his blue eyes were clear and bright. Angela decided that if he wore a sailor cap and jacket he would fit perfectly in the picture on a box of frozen fish.

Shyly, the two girls sat down.

"Now, Captain, you didn't really have to make a trip up here just to adopt a kitten," Mrs. Seegal said.

"Well, ma'am, I don't usually call myself Captain anymore, now that I'm retired. Just plain Angus will do, though the folks around here seem to like to hang the 'Captain' moniker on me."

"You're retired?"

"Yes, forcibly retired." He sighed. "I was captain of one of the ferries to the Island—" he broke off. "Sorry, I mean Prince Edward Island. I keep forgetting that for people here, 'Island' means Cape Breton. Anyway, when the bridge to PEI was built, the ferries were sold off and I was offered early retirement, so my wife and I decided to take it and move somewhere quieter. The island I live on now was once in her family, so we bought it back and moved there. I built us a cottage, winterized for year-round living and all. We were there for about two years before Mary fell ill, and then she passed away a year later."

"I'm so sorry to hear that," said Mrs. Seegal.

"Well, they were still three happy years for her and me. And I've really grown to love this part of the Maritimes. The folks around Mahone Bay, they make it easier to bear—her leaving me. So now I'm on the island alone, and I don't mind most of the time, but your ad got me thinking that maybe a cat would be good company. It might even put a scare into the mice trying to raid my pantry."

"Are you often away from the island?" Emmie asked, worried about Rascal being left alone.

"Not usually more than a day. Most times I go into town for supplies or a chat with Alister, or to get a meal I don't have to rustle up myself. Cooking's pretty good here. I like to get a sandwich at the lunch counter at William's—reminds me of when I was a boy, climbing up on those stools. But for a good meal nothing beats the café. Have you eaten there?"

At this the other three laughed uproariously. When they caught their breath, they explained to the bewildered captain that Emmie's mother was one of the cooks at the aforementioned café. That got him chuckling at his unknowing compliment. Angela was finding him very easy to like; he seemed so honest and kind. She wondered if Emmie felt the same way.

"Now, I don't know what other details of my life you need to know in order to consider me as a parent for Mr. Kitten here." He looked down, and it was only then that the girls realized that Rascal had snuck up into a fold of the Captain's jacket and was fast asleep.

"Well, that's the longest he's been still since we found him in the attic," said Emmie's mother. "The girls were having a little poetic license with this 'adoption' notice they put in the paper, and wanting to interview prospective owners."

"But Mom, we were serious!" Emmie interjected.

Before her mother could argue, Captain Targus broke in. "Quite right, you know. There are, unfortunately, too many irresponsible people taking on pets these days, and I agree you should get to know the person you are going to entrust your precious bundle with for the next fifteen years or so."

"Well, that's what they do with people who're adopting a child." Emmie looked firmly at her mother. "I'm sure you and Dad were carefully checked out before they gave me to you, weren't you?" She didn't see Angela's startled look.

"Yes, dear," replied her mother, resigning herself to losing yet another verbal battle with her daughter. "Well, is there anything else you want to ask our guest?"

"No, not really. I appreciate you coming all the way out here just for a kitten," said Emmie.

"Oh, it was no trouble at all. I was in town for groceries today and I did so want to meet the people who created such an intriguing ad." At that Captain Targus rose and handed Rascal to Emmie. "Here, you had better take him back—I'm liable to sneak off with him. By the way, does he have a name?"

"Rascal! He's just a little punk, always getting into trouble." Emmie was almost proud of Rascal's reputation, but suddenly remembered who she was talking to. "I expect he'll settle down when he grows up, though."

"Well, that's as good a name as any. I'm a great believer in names that fit, and if that's his reputation already, then Rascal it is. Now please do tell me tomorrow if I'm approved to adopt him. You can call Alister and he'll radio me; there's no telephone line to the island so I make do with 'ship-to-shore' radio. You said you knew Alister, didn't you?" Captain Targus began to walk toward the front door.

"Just about everyone around here knows Alister," Emmie's mother replied, walking with the Captain. "He's often put our boat into the water and taken it out with my husband when he's home. And he trims our trees, too." She opened the front door. "Thank you for indulging these two girls' imaginations, Mr. Targus."

They watched and waved as the Captain drove Alister's car down the lane to the highway.

"I didn't know you were adopted!" exclaimed Angela when they had retired to Emmie's room. "I mean, if that isn't too personal." She paused, embarrassed. "Am I being nosy?"

"Nah. I've always known I was adopted. Where'd you think this red hair comes from? Mom and Dad are dark, and so was Gram. Being adopted is just a part of me—but then, it isn't. Know what I mean?"

Angela nodded, even though she wasn't quite sure what Emmie meant at all. Emmie seemed to sense Angela's confusion, and continued.

"It's like…I guess it's important because I'm different, I'm ME. And it's not important where I come from, because this is my home and these are my parents, and there's nobody else in this world that can ever be that!"

Angela thought about it for a minute. She had never thought of her parents and her home in that way. What would it be like having another past, another beginning? She couldn't really get her head around that one.

Her thoughts turned to the captain they had just met, and his sad past. Would he give Rascal a happy home like she and Emmie had?

"What do you think about the Captain?" Angela said. "Will he be a good parent for our baby?"

"Yeah, I think he will. He seems pretty nice, and he's lonely, too. You could see it in his eyes when he talked about his wife dying and everything. What did Eleanor say about him again?"

"Hmm," Angela thought for a moment. "She said he comes into William's for a bite to eat, but she suspects it's more for the conversation and socializing around the lunch counter."

"That's so sad about his wife," Emmie looked thoughtful. "Eleanor said that when she got sick she wouldn't come off the island except to go to the Bridgewater Hospital. She loved being on the island so much she wouldn't go and live in town for the winter, even though it was way closer to the hospital."

"And then she died last spring in Captain Targus's arms, just as the doctor was arriving." Angela felt her eyes getting misty. "I can see why he'd be lonely."

With a loud meow, Rascal pushed the bedroom door open, bounced into the room, and jumped up onto the bed between the girls, as if to say, "Was someone talking about me?" The girls laughed.

"So," asked Angela, "are we decided?"

"I think he'd make a good parent," said Emmie. "We'll call Alister in the morning and he can radio Captain Targus."

CHAPTER 8
The Island

The next morning Emmie called Alister. After listening for a long time she said goodbye, hung up the phone, and turned to Angela. She did not look happy at all.

"What's wrong?" Angela looked worried. "Won't he take Rascal?"

"No, it's not that. Alister says the Captain's boat started breaking down on his way back to the island and he just got it there before the motor died. The part he needs won't be in town for at least a week and that means he can't come and get Rascal. I guess we could keep him for another week, but he's getting bigger by the day and he's getting into more and more trouble."

Just then there was a crash from the kitchen. The girls rushed in to find a flower vase about to roll off the counter, with water and daisies streaming to the floor and Rascal scooting under the stove.

"See what I mean?" Emmie said as she rushed to rescue the vase. She mopped up all the water while Angela gathered the flowers. Rascal, thinking the coast was clear, came out and rubbed himself against Angela's legs.

"You are so naughty, Rascal. It's a good thing Emmie's mom isn't here right now or you'd be swimming out to Captain Targus."

"Hey," said Emmie, "that gives me an idea." She walked back out to the phone in the front hall, leaving Angela to finish putting the bouquet back together.

When Mrs. Seegal arrived home from the breakfast shift a half-hour later, she was greeted with the news. She didn't look happy at the prospect of another week of kitten mayhem.

"Mom, I have a solution." Emmie looked hopeful. "Why don't you let me and Angela take our boat over to the island and deliver Rascal to Captain Targus?"

"Absolutely not! Have you taken leave of your senses? That boat is too heavy for a little girl to operate."

"Mom! I'm almost thirteen, and Angela is twelve. And Dad already taught me how to run the boat; he lets me drive it all the time."

"He does, does he? Well, that's news to me."

"Honest, Mom. He didn't tell you last summer 'cause you're always afraid of me being on the water. But it's a calm day, and the island isn't that far from the wharf, and we could get Rascal settled and—"

"All right, that's enough." Her mother thought for a minute, then sighed. "I keep forgetting that you're growing up, Emily. I guess we could put the boat in the water for when your father comes back, and...I suppose you can take it out to the island with the kitten for a short while," she said, looking sternly at Emmie, "*if* Alister feels you check out on handling the boat."

"YEAH!" Both girls jumped up, sending Rascal scurrying back under the stove.

"But if Alister doesn't think you can handle it, then he has to go with you."

Strangely enough, Alister was at the farm with his truck in less than an hour to hitch up the boat and trailer, and soon they were jouncing down the road in his truck with Rascal in Bootsie's cat carrier on Angela's lap.

"How did you get here so fast?" asked Angela.

Alister smiled. "A little bird told me you'd be putting the boat in the water," he grinned. "A little red-haired bird."

Soon he was backing the boat down the ramp next to the government wharf. Emmie hopped out of the cab and grabbed a hockey bag from the truck box, while Alister filled the boat's gas tank. Emmie unzipped the bag and handed Angela a life vest, putting one on herself, too. Then she pulled out a can of compressed air and screwed it onto the pipe that connected to the air horn. Finally, she unfolded a Canadian flag and clipped it to the flagstaff on the stern.

When Alister had dropped the freshly charged battery into its case and attached the cables, Emmie moved to the stern, pulled the safety clip from the motor housing, and easily lowered the big engine into the water as if she had done this all her life.

"Well, she's fit as a fiddle, Miss Emily. Your papa keeps his boat in first-class shape. By the way, where is he right now?"

"Somewhere off the coast of Portugal, according to his last letter, and from there they've got a cargo for Britain, where he'll either be discharged and flown home, or he'll pick up with a new crew to cross the Atlantic." Emmie paused, putting her hands on her hips and addressing Alister in a mock-serious tone: "Well, Mr. McLean, do we check out to go to sea?"

"Boat's all checked out, ma'am, but you're only checked out as far as that island over there." Alister pointed to the hazy hump out past the point. "Remember, even though the mainland is relatively close to one shore of the island, the other coast is open to the sea. Keep to the windward side, and you'll see the Captain's jetty. You can't miss the *Lady Mary* at anchor there. He keeps it so clean it hurts your eyes to look at it. Now, I'll cast you off and radio the Captain that you're on the way."

Angela looked across the bay to the far shore. Her house stood halfway up the hill, gleaming in the sunlight, and the roof of Emmie's house just poked out of the trees at the top of the hill. A little farther down the road, at the water's edge, was a small wooden wharf running out from a stone pier, common property for the families that lived there. That's where the boat was moored last summer when she first met Emmie, but Emmie's father had shipped out soon after, and Emmie had not been allowed to take the boat anywhere.

Alister pushed them off and Emmie settled herself in the bow. She turned on the ignition switch and pushed a red button. With a roar the big outboard sprang to life, belching smoky exhaust for a moment, then settling down to a low rumble. Emmie pushed the gear lever into forward and opened the throttle slowly. The grey boat—which seemed so big to Angela, sitting deep inside it, but was so much smaller than the fine cruisers in the bay—slowly swung into the channel and turned its bow out to sea.

Meow, MEOW! Rascal was not a happy sailor in his carry cage on Angela's lap. *Merrow.* He pushed his nose against the door of the cage. Angela made soothing noises as the engine noise grew louder. Now that they were clear of the wharf, Emmie accelerated the boat. Slowly the bow rose up on the water and the boat started to spit spray at them. Soon they were roaring out to sea. Emmie kept her hands firmly on the wheel, enjoying the rush of the wind through her flaming curls. Angela had never been outside the bay in this big a boat before, and was beginning to like it. Even Rascal settled down and folded himself up on the blanket in the bottom of the carrier for a nap.

On they sped, across sparkling wavelets, watching gulls dip and glide and cormorants plunge into the water and come up with fish in their beaks. Back on the shore they could see an osprey heading to her nest, and for a moment they thought they saw a bald eagle disappear into the tall fir trees that crowded along the shore and marched back for miles inland.

All too soon, it seemed, the island grew larger and larger and Emmie throttled back the engine. They slowly circled around the back of the island and saw the jetty with the white motor boat tied up to it. As they got nearer, Angela found herself holding her breath. Above them loomed the most beautiful cruiser she had ever seen. It was sparkling white, with colourful signal flags hanging from the radio antenna wires and a large Canadian flag flapping idly from the stern. Every piece of brass railing shone and the teak woodwork gleamed. As they drew alongside a cheerful voice called to them from above.

"Ahoy, ladies, welcome!" The trim figure of Captain Targus leaned over the boat's railing. "Just a minute, I'll come down and get your painter."

Angela looked at Emmie, confused.

"The painter is the rope for tying the boat up," Emmie whispered.

Soon their whaler was tied up at the wharf, and they were accompanying the Captain, carrying the cat, up a stone path to a trim log cabin set in a grove of red pine trees. Like the boat, the cabin was as neat as could be. The logs were stained and varnished, and when he ushered them in, it was into a snug, tidy, cozy interior.

"Welcome to my humble abode," said Captain Targus, looking around his home. "Now, shall we close the door and release Mr. Rascal from his imprisonment?"

It only took a minute for Rascal to venture out of the cat carrier and start inspecting the cabin. They were in a large room with a wooden table and four chairs, with a galley kitchen off to one side. A comfy living room extended from the kitchen area down to two more rooms at the end of the cabin. The chairs and couch were neat and comfortable, and soon the girls were relaxing in them with a cold drink while Rascal made his inspection.

"I think he approves," commented Emmie.

Merrow, answered Rascal. *ME-RROW!*

"Oh my gosh!" exclaimed Emmie, putting down her drink. She rushed down to the dock, returning a moment later with the hockey bag. From it she produced a water dish, food bowl, litter box and a bag of cat litter. Finally she drew out two tins of Rascal's favourite cat food.

Merrow, merrow! Rascal grew insistent and frantic, getting in everyone's way as they set up his feeding place and opened the can. Soon he had his face buried in the dish and quiet returned.

"Well, he seems quite at home here," observed Captain Targus. Rascal finished up his meal, took a long drink, and then strolled over to where they were sitting. He looked at Angela. He looked at Emmie. Then, with a leap, he landed on the Captain's lap, purring and kneading gently.

"If I had any worries about how he'd adapt, they're gone now. Will you be letting him outside, Captain Targus?" Emmie asked.

"Gradually. I'll make sure he knows where home is, and then he can roam. The island is only lightly wooded; it was burnt over about forty years ago, so there isn't a lot of heavy undergrowth. A cat can move easily about and still see and be seen, so he shouldn't have any trouble finding his dinner dish. Anyway, it's an island, so he can't go too far, unless he likes to swim."

"Not a chance! He hates getting wet, even when he just knocks over a flower vase."

Just then a radio crackled in one of the rooms off the living room. "Pointer calling Targus, Pointer calling Targus." The Captain got up quickly and led them to a small study with a neat desk that looked out on the water through a blue-curtained window. Beside the desk was an assortment of radio gear with a speaker hung on the wall and a microphone on the table.

"Angus here. Come in, Alister," the Captain called into the mic.

"Hello, you old salt. Are the girls still there?" came Alister's voice over the speaker.

"Snug and sound."

"It's getting on, Angus, and there's a warning for a fast-moving storm coming up the coast later this evening, so I think they should be motoring home soon."

"Good idea, though I was just getting used to the company. Thanks for the warning, Alister. I have them set sail shortly. You can let their parents know. Over and out."

"I copy. Over and out."

"Well," Captain Targus sighed, "It seems our

visit is all too short. Perhaps you can come over some other time and check out Mr. Kitten and see how he's doing."

"Oh, we'd love to," replied Angela, with Emmie nodding her agreement beside her.

By now they were walking down the path to the dock. The *Lady Mary* rocked gently at anchor, the wind snapping its flags. Angela noticed that there was more wind than when they landed, but the water was still calm. They said their goodbyes as the engine started. Soon they were headed out of the little cove that housed the Captain's wharf and back to town.

Once they were clear of the island the water grew a bit rougher, but the sky was still clear and the sun shone. Emmie looked at her watch. "Uh-oh, it's nearly four. We really stayed too long." She notched the throttle forward and the boat leapt through the waves. The rolling seas thumped under the boat and the pelting spray was getting a bit uncomfortable.

On they motored, the island now just a misty lump behind them and the lighthouse on the point not yet visible. The air grew colder, and the sun started to duck behind dark clouds that were moving quickly across the sea. Angela glanced at Emmie. She was gripping the wheel more tightly and staring tensely out over the water. A few drops of rain started to spit on them, then becoming a spatter, and soon a steady drizzle. The wind picked up at the same time and the water grew rougher. Emmie throttled back slightly, but the boat still hit each wave with an alarming thump.

Suddenly the dark clouds rushed down at them, the sky opened up, and the rain poured, soaking them in an instant. Then an almighty crack of thunder signalled that the storm wasn't waiting for evening—it was here, and they were still far from land and safety.

CHAPTER 9

Storm

The wind howled in Angela's ears as the sea and the rain drenched her. She could only tell which it was when she licked her lips—if it was salty, she had just been hit with another wave. Emmie shouted to her to hang on, but she was already clutching the lifeline that ran the length of each side of the boat with a death grip.

"Come up forward!" Emmie shouted over the gale.

Angela inched her way hand over hand towards her and finally slid into the other seat beside the helm. Emmie nodded to a seat strap, and Angela buckled herself in. Emmie was holding the wheel as tightly as possible, trying with every wave to keep the whaler on a steady course. Rain poured down and Angela wondered if the boat would fill, but Emmie practically read her mind, shouting, "There's an automatic bailer on the motor, and so far it's keeping up."

The seas rose and fell like a crazy roller coaster. Spray mixed with rain and washed over the windshield and into the cockpit. Every so often a jag of lightning broke through the black sky, followed closely by a deafening crash of thunder. The poor flag snapped at its clips, drenched like a dish rag. From time to time the motor roared frighteningly loudly as the propeller came right out of the water for a moment on the crest of a wave.

Angela was scared stiff. She glanced over. Emmie kept her grip on the wheel and her eyes on the horizon.

"Can you see anything?" Emmie shouted.

Angela strained her eyes hopefully. Of the two she had the sharper vision, and could usually pick out details far sooner than Emmie. But that didn't help her now—all she could see was the angry grey ocean. "Nothing yet," she shouted, trying to be heard over the howling of the wind and the engine.

They motored on, smashing into each wave, being lifted up by a roller and slammed down into the trough, then up again over the next one. Angela worried whether even such a heavy, well-built craft could continue to take a pounding like this.

On and on they went. The fury of the storm didn't let up one bit. It seemed to Angela that they should be near the wharf by now. What if Emmie had miscalculated? What if they had turned right around and were headed out to sea? What if the engine were to quit? All these thoughts ran through her mind as she clung to the side of the cockpit to keep her head from being slammed into the windshield.

She glanced over at Emmie. Never had she seen such a look of sheer determination on her friend's face. Emmie's jaw was set, her hands white from gripping the steering wheel. Her hair was a mass of sodden curls and her breath came in short sharp jabs as she wrestled the boat from wave to wave. If she was scared, she didn't have time to show it.

But Angela was the most scared she had ever been in her life. Her stomach flipped with the boat's rise and fall, her pulse was racing and she felt sick. But she knew she had to keep on looking. Her eyes ached with sweat, rain and salt water as she scanned the rolling horizon. The black curtain of rain made every point she looked at identical to the last, just a blur of grey that could be coastline or could be open ocean.

Then something caught her eye. She strained to catch it again as the boat rose and fell. Now it was gone. Was it just the lightning? She kept looking in the same direction, even though she felt like she was going to throw up at any moment if she kept watching the horizon weave and bob, up and down.

There it was again, something tiny and bright yellow in the grey of the rain.

"There, over to your right, there's something yellow! Over there! Do you see it?"

Emmie shook her head.

"It's over there! Steer for it!"

Emmie looked where Angela was pointing, and with great difficulty turned the wheel in that direction. The yellow disappeared, then Angela saw it again.

"I think it might be my mom in her yellow rain slicker. She must be on the wharf. Head for it."

Emmie nodded. Now she could see the minuscule dot of yellow poking out of the grey, rain-swept landscape. Slowly the horizon grew closer. It was land! Now and again they could see a wisp of pine trees through the curtain of heavy rain. Slowly the sea swells eased as the boat came closer to the land. Once more they saw the flash of yellow, far ahead of them. Emmie set a course for it as it disappeared again.

The pounding rain lessened slightly, though the storm's fury was still around them. Emmie steered carefully, trying to keep the shore in sight, but not so close as to get them swept up in the waves and smashed on the rocks that defined the South Shore of Nova Scotia.

The pitching and rolling was really getting to Angela. Her eyes swam, her stomach refused to sit still, and she was bitterly cold. Then all of a sudden the swells dropped and the wind backed off a bit.

"We must be into the harbour!" Emmie yelled, steering the boat toward the spot where they had seen the yellow slicker. A moment later the rain parted and the wind died completely, and in a few minutes the familiar, weathered wooden wharf ran out to meet them. Soon the boat was tied up and they were staggering across the worn boards and collapsing onto the dock, exhausted.

After a few minutes, Angela finally sat up. She looked around them. The wharf was already starting to dry in places, as if there had only been a light shower here—the storm had bypassed

Mahone Bay. They pulled off their soaked life vests and slowly dragged their weary legs up the slope, across the road and up the hill to Angela's house.

"Oh my goodness," said Angela's mother when she saw them. "Where have you been?"

After the girls explained, very briefly, they changed into some of Angela's dry clothes. Back downstairs, Angela's mother told them that there had only been a slight shower around Mahone Bay.

"It was a good thing you put on your yellow slicker and came down to the dock to look for us," said Angela. "Otherwise we would never have found our way back."

Her mother looked at her strangely. "What yellow slicker?"

"The one in the hall closet."

"Oh, that one. I don't know why I bought it; it doesn't fit and I never wear it."

The two girls looked at each other in amazement.

Angela finally spoke. "But—you were wearing it when you came to look for us, right?"

"What? I told you, it was just a light shower here and I wasn't worried. I certainly didn't come down to the wharf to look for you. Why do you ask?"

"Because I saw it through the rain, and someone was wearing it, and it's way too small for Matt or Dad, and they're both working today anyway, so I thought it must have been you."

"You must be imagining things."

"Mom, I saw someone wearing a yellow slicker standing on the wharf, and when they saw us, they went back into the brush, up to the road."

"Well, dear, it wasn't me."

"Then what did I see?"

"I really don't know, dear—maybe a yellow sign on the road? I'm glad you saw something, though. Thank goodness you made it back safely."

With the puzzle running through their heads, Angela and Emmie retired to Angela's room with mugs of hot chocolate.

"There's no yellow sign anywhere on that stretch of the road," said Emmie. "I should know, I've walked it enough times."

"So…what did we see?" Angela asked meekly, almost reluctant to hear the answer.

"I don't know. Where's your mom's slicker?"

"In the front hall closet."

"And she never wears it?"

"Well, you heard her."

They looked at each other as they had the same thought, ran down the stairs and opened the closet door. The yellow raincoat hung from a peg at the back. Emmie took it off the peg and handed it to Angela, who could see immediately that it was more her size than her mother's. And it was perfectly dry.

"Another mystery, I guess," said Emmie, taking it and putting it back on the peg.

Angela wondered if Emmie had noticed that, although the coat was dry, the lining was warm inside, as if it had just been worn. Her mind was racing as she led Emmie back upstairs.

CHAPTER 10

Mysteries Debated

"I still don't believe there's any such thing as ghosts. There's just no proof!" Emmie rolled over on her back and stared up at the fluffy clouds drifting high above Angela's front yard. After sleeping at Angela's house the night before, they had been arguing most of the afternoon about the existence of spirits.

Angela was propped up on her elbows looking out over the bay. Off to their left, Spook was chasing white butterflies. She thought for a minute about what Emmie said, then spoke.

"I never told you, but I saw something in your attic when we found Spook."

"What?" said Emmie excitedly, sitting up.

"There was something like a mist standing at the top of the stairs. It almost looked like a person in a long white nightgown, and then it was gone."

"I think your imagination was working overtime. Too many of those ghost books on your poor tired brain." Emmie threw a handful of grass at Angela, who chose to ignore it.

"And what about the yellow raincoat waiting for us in the storm? What could that have been except a ghost?"

"Maybe it was your mom, but she doesn't want you to know she was worrying. My mother always pretends she doesn't wait by the window and watch for me to come home."

"No, my mom's not like that. If she said she wasn't there, then she wasn't there." Angela spoke with finality.

Spook, tired of running around, wandered over to where they were sitting and settled herself into Angela's lap.

"I still think that all we heard was that cat on the stairs." Emmie nodded her head toward Spook.

"Do you really believe that a kitten could have crawled out of the box, across the whole attic floor and down those stairs, when it could barely stand on those wobbly legs?" Angela stroked the soft white fur and Spook purred approvingly.

Emmie looked pensive, but didn't answer.

"And make all that noise?" Angela continued.

"Spook isn't even heavy enough now to make that loud a thump." She hoisted the kitten in the air as if to weigh it.

"Maybe it seemed louder 'cause it was so quiet late at night." Emmie chewed on a long piece of grass as she tried to come up with a logical explanation. "And kittens are tougher than they seem, it's their survival adaptation that we learned about in science class."

"And the person in the yellow slicker?"

"Sheesh, Angela, I don't know." She threw away the piece of grass in exasperation. "Maybe you saw a yellow plastic bag caught on a branch. That might be why it kept disappearing—it was flapping in the wind and then it blew away."

Angela thought for a long time. The sun was warm, the air still. Down on the water they could see boats moving slowly in and out of the harbour. Tourist season was in full swing and every day brought new sleek cruisers and sailing boats into the bay.

Eventually she got up and deposited the kitten in Emmie's arms while she stretched. "I still think we have a guardian angel or ghost or whatever you want to call it. Otherwise those kittens might never have been found." She shivered at the thought. "And we might have never gotten home last night. Explain it any way you want, Emmie, I'll stick to my ghosts."

They started up the porch steps, deposited Spook inside, and poured themselves two glasses of lemonade from the fridge. Kicking back in the comfy chairs on the porch, they watched the boats, the ospreys, and the gulls.

Summer's a great time to be alive, thought Angela. Despite their harrowing adventure coming back from the island, Emmie's mom had grudgingly admitted that Emmie really knew how to handle the whaler. And she had finally said that they would be allowed to take it out again—though they were to first check the weather channel, please.

But was there any such thing as a ghost? The books Angela was reading clearly stated that people had actually seen these apparitions. And it wasn't her imagination the night they found the kittens. She had seen something real, as real as a spirit could be. It was a woman, or older girl, dressed in a white, flowing sort of dress. It had stood there for a moment, as if making sure that the kitten was safe, then it had vanished.

And the person at the wharf? Again, it was a woman. She had stood there only long enough to make sure Angela and Emmie were okay. If it were the same angel or spirit, then it was a kindly one that was looking out for them. Angela sighed. Whatever else it was, it was definitely a mystery. And there was one thing she knew for sure: Even though Emmie didn't believe in ghosts, she loved a mystery. That promised to keep this debate alive for the rest of the summer.

CHAPTER 11

Another Visit

Days slipped into weeks as the strawberries ripened in Emmie's garden. The osprey babies had hatched and the girls spent endless days watching the parents teach their young to fish. Sometimes gulls would chase the young osprey and knock the fish from their talons. It was hard to say who was more indignant, the osprey or the two friends watching.

Spook grew and grew—helped, no doubt, by Angela's mother sneaking her scraps from the table despite Angela and her dad's disapproval. Bootsie had almost forgiven Emmie for taking her kittens, and the summer was settling into a warm, drowsy routine of having fun, eating snacks, dozing on the lawn with a book, and waiting for lunch or supper.

And, of course, there were trips into town, ice cream at William's, and the ever-changing parade of sailboats and motorboats in and out of the bay. Many of them flew flags from other nations, mostly the United States, but there were boats visiting from Germany, France, and Britain, as well.

But of all the motorboats that crowded the snug harbour—and there were many finely outfitted ones—none could hold a candle to the *Lady Mary* when it came to town. The Captain loved his boat, though he was no show-off, and the *Lady* shone brilliantly as a result of his loving care. The correct pennants flew from its mast, the right signal flags from the radio wires (usually "Welcome Aboard"), and its engine always purred like a satisfied kitten.

Sometimes the girls were lucky enough to be in town when Captain Targus docked, and he always had time to update them on Rascal's latest adventures or mishaps. Often he'd suggest they discuss their mutual cat friend over a dish of ice cream at William's. Angela noticed, though, that no matter how many scoops the girls had, the Captain only ever had a small dish, plain vanilla.

It was on one such day, with their legs dangling from the chrome and red-leather stools, spooning their ice cream from heavy glass dishes, that Angus (as he insisted they call him) suggested they might like to visit the island again and see how Rascal had grown. The girls were excited at the prospect, despite their troubles the last time. After negotiating with their respective parents, they decided that—weather permitting—they'd visit the Captain the following Monday.

The day was fine, and both the weather channel and marine radio promised a light breeze and clear skies. The whaler motored along, skipping over the waves as Angela enjoyed the feeling of spray and breeze on her face. It was an antidote of sorts for the horrible voyage of a few weeks ago, which had faded a bit in their memories. The tree-rimmed shore slipped away and the familiar hump of the island grew slowly larger. Emmie deftly turned the whaler so they could circle the island before coming to the wharf. The island was a fair size, about as big as Emmie's parents' farm. Most of it was covered in forest, primarily pines, but at one spot there was a dilapidated old stone jetty, and on a hill poking through the trees was a ruined stone chimney, the remnants of someone else's life there.

Eventually they rounded the back of the island and approached the wharf. The *Lady Mary* swung slowly at its moorings, flags hanging limp in the still air. No one greeted them, but they supposed that Captain Targus was out walking the paths that led through the island brush, as he said he often did.

They tied up the whaler and started up the path to the cabin. Angela pushed open the door.

"Hello! Anybody home?" she called as she closed it behind them.

Merrow, answered a voice from the dusky interior, and in a moment a sleek brown-and-black Rascal bounced out of the bedroom and into Emmie's arms.

"Oh my, what a handsome cat you are," she murmured. "You were right, Angela, he's grown up to be bigger than either of the others."

"Now, where's the Captain?" asked Angela. She stepped to a window and called "Hello?" but only the shrill cry of a blue jay answered.

"Where's Angus?" Emmie said jokingly to the purring cat in her arms.

Merrow. He jumped down and pawed the cabin door. *Meow!*

"Do you think it's all right to let him out?"

"I think so. Angus says he lets him out all the time now."

Angela opened the door and Rascal took off like a shot down the path to the dock, the two girls following close behind. At the dock he hesitated, then cautiously started toward the gangway of the *Lady Mary*.

"Angus must be on the boat," said Emmie, "but why didn't he come out when we docked?"

Rascal pawed the gangway as if he were afraid to walk over the water lapping below. *Merrrrow, merrrrow,* he called plaintively. Angela scooped him up and they mounted the gangway.

The deck of the boat was as spotless as the kitchen at the café. Every teak plank gleamed and there was not a speck of dirt to be seen. Brass railings and portholes winked in the sun, and everything that wasn't brass or teak was blindingly white.

The boat creaked as it rode a small swell. A gull cried somewhere over the island. Otherwise it was ghostly quiet.

"Halloo," Angela called.

"Hello, Angus, are you here?" Emmie echoed.

No one answered.

Merrow! Suddenly Rascal clawed his way out of Angela's grip and darted down the deck toward the bow.

"Come back, Rascal, you'll fall in!" they shouted, running after him. He streaked ahead, rounded the wheelhouse and disappeared from view. The girls rounded the corner after him and stopped cold.

On the deck, with a paintbrush still clutched in his hand, lay Angus. Rascal stood by him, rubbing against him. The girls rushed forward.

Angela knelt beside Angus. All her CPR training came back to her in a rush. She quickly felt for a pulse. Yes, it was there, but not very strong. She placed her ear near the Captain's mouth.

"He's breathing, but I think he's out cold."

"I can't see a lump or anything. Try waking him up." Emmie was kneeling on the other side.

"Captain Targus, can you hear me? Angus! Can you hear me?"

There was no answer. Emmie ran into the wheelhouse, found a cloth and wetted it. They bathed the Captain's brow, but there was still no response. Angela tried his pulse again. It was still beating, but it was still weak.

"He must be in some sort of coma!" Angela straightened up. "Is there a radio in the boat? We'll have to call for help."

Emmie looked anxiously into the wheelhouse. There was a maze of electronic equipment, dials and gauges and a microphone, but she couldn't make out what belonged to what.

"I'm afraid to start turning anything on," she said nervously.

"See if there's a switch on the microphone." Angela knelt by the Captain again.

Emmie searched frantically. "I can't see anything that turns the radio on! Maybe it's only on when the engine is running."

"What about the radio back in the cabin?"

"I know as much about radios as flying to the moon." Emmie was starting to sound panicky.

"Me too." Angela was becoming desperate. "We'd better get him into the whaler and go to town for help."

Angus wasn't a big man, but the two girls struggled to carry his limp form across the cruiser's deck. They carefully manoeuvred him down the steep gangplank, trying not to let him be bumped by the stanchions. Once they had to put him down and catch their breath—just for a moment—as they lugged him across the wharf. Finally they lowered the Captain as gently as they could onto one of the boat's seats, and tucked him against the padded seat back. Angela whipped off her jacket and rolled it into a pillow while Emmie unfastened the painter and jumped in.

The engine roared to life and Emmie jammed the gearshift forward so quickly the gears crunched. She rammed the throttle forward and the whaler leapt up in the sea, rushing away from the dock. Quickly they left the island behind, as they headed at full speed toward Mahone Bay, and help.

CHAPTER 12

An Unknown Helper

On and on the boat roared over the water. The lighthouse at the tip of Mahone Bay slowly grew larger—too slowly for Angela. She checked on Angus, lying still on the bottom of the boat. He was still breathing, still unconscious.

Finally, after what seemed like an eternity, the lighthouse island swung by them and they entered the long, wide bay. There was still a lot of open water to cross, and in the distance Angela could just see a dark smudge that she knew was the government wharf. Eventually the huge concrete shape shook itself loose from the green haze that was the shoreline. Now it was easier to see the imposing structure, which was higher than a tall adult at high tide and twice that at what was now nearly low tide. Emmie throttled back just enough to prevent an accident as she wove between the boats moored out in the deep part of the bay. Finally she cleared the moorings and headed toward the wharf's launch ramp. Angela noticed that more than the usual scattering of people were clustered along the front of the wharf and wondered what was happening. When they saw Emmie's boat racing toward them, several people ran across the wharf, over to the ramp, and down into the water to meet them.

In a minute, strong hands were grabbing at the whaler, steadying it as Emmie cut the engine, then Doc Cruson pushed his way through the crowd, wading into the water with his black bag. He took a quick, careful look at the Captain, then opened his bag, took out a needle, and gave Angus an injection. The girls jumped out of the boat into the water to hold it and keep it from floating away, and at that same moment the ambulance from Bridgewater Hospital screamed its way up to the ramp. Doc and the ambulance attendant quickly lifted the Captain onto a stretcher, carried him up the ramp, and loaded him into the ambulance. Before the girls could even ask any questions, Doc jumped in the back with the stretcher, the ambulance doors slammed shut, and the siren started to wail again as the ambulance raced away.

Angela and Emmie stood waist-deep in the water, open-mouthed and confused about where everyone had come from and what had just happened. Then Alister appeared at their side and grabbed the whaler's painter.

"You lasses get up to the truck while I tie her up. You've had too much excitement today to be sailing anywhere else." He gently took the rope out of Emmie's hand.

Stunned by what had just happened, and dripping wet, they obeyed, slowly walking up the ramp and climbing into the broad front seat of Alister's truck to wait for him.

"There now." Alister slid into the truck and started the engine. "That was a very brave thing for you two to do. Doc says he'll be okay with that shot of insulin. Angus is diabetic, did you know?"

The truck moved slowly down Main Street and Angela felt as if everyone was turning to look at them. She and Emmie were silent for what felt like a long time, still shaken by the wild ride and everything that had happened afterward. Finally, Angela spoke.

"No. I didn't know. But that explains why he always eats such a small dish of ice cream, doesn't it?"

"Aye. He was able to keep it under control by watching his diet, but I suspect he had slipped into a diabetic coma when you found him. I'd say he owes his life to you. Now, tell me," Alister continued, "how did you two manage to work that old radio in the cabin to call ahead for the Doc?" Angela and Emmie looked at each other in amazement, but Alister, his eyes on the road, didn't notice. "Such an antique, that radio," he continued. "I've been at him for ages to get a new one. Takes a bleeding engineer to figure it out."

"Um, we didn't use the cabin radio." Angela found she had to force the words out, she was so shocked at what Alister had just said.

"Oh, of course you didn't! Silly me. You must have radioed me from the *Lady Mary*." Angus slowed down for a woman with a small baby trying to cross Main Street.

"We did what?" Emmie asked, startled.

Alister turned onto the highway. "I was passing by the radio room at the back of my place—you know, the old spare bedroom—and I heard 'mayday,' real faint with a lot of static." He paused while he changed gears to climb the hill leading out of town. "So of course I got right into the room and caught you saying 'Angus is in a coma…coming to town.' So I called Doc and the ambulance in

Bridgewater, and set off for the wharf and there you were. Right fast you made it, too, coming in no more than twenty-five minutes after you called." He chuckled at the thought. "Miss Emmie, you're gonna be a speedboat racer if you keep drivin' like that."

"But..." Angela started to say, but Emmie jabbed her in the ribs. The two girls looked at Alister, but he was still just looking at the road. Emmie looked at Angela and put her finger to her lips. Then she shook her head as if to say, "I don't understand either, but let's not talk about it here." Angela looked at her watch. They had left Mason's Island over forty minutes ago. Something didn't add up, but she was fatigued from the ride and excitement, too wet and chilled to think about it any further.

Alister had turned down Indian Road, heading for Angela's place. "It's a good thing Angus had the radio switched on in his boat." He resumed his explanation now that they were out of town traffic. "Usually he leaves it off unless he's motoring; it soaks up battery power like crazy."

Both girls sat in shocked silence, not sure what to say next. Soon the truck swung into Angela's driveway and up the steep hill.

"Well, here you are, Angela." Alister stopped the truck where the driveway came up to the back door. "Miss Emmie, do you want a ride to your place?"

Emmie shook her head. "No, it's all right, I'll walk." Her voice sounded strangely remote as she opened her door, still in a daze.

Angela started to slide across the seat to get out.

"That's fine," said Alister. "I'll be heading over to Bridgewater then, to see Captain at the hospital. I'm sure they'll want to keep him in for observation for a few days."

"Rascal!" both girls suddenly shouted in alarm.

"What?" asked the confused Alister.

"Angus's cat that we gave him," Emmie wailed. "He'll starve 'cause we closed the cabin door when he led us to the boat, and his food is inside the cabin and—"

"Now, calm down," said Alister soothingly. "I'll check up on the Captain, and then, if you don't mind, I'll take your whaler over to the island and feed puss. Okay?"

"Oh, that would be great." Emmie breathed a sigh of relief and relaxed.

"Can you please call us and tell us if Angus is all right?" Angela looked at Alister anxiously.

"Of course I will. Now, you get yourselves dried off." And with that Alister turned the truck in the driveway and started back down the hill, leaving two very confused girls standing in wet shoes, socks, and shorts. Their heads were buzzing with questions, but they wondered if there were even any answers.

CHAPTER 13

Mysteries, Mysteries

"Ghosts don't use marine radio!" Emmie stated it with such finality that it startled Angela. They were sitting in Emmie's kitchen, snacking on fresh strawberries from her garden and going over the events of the day before. Alister had phoned last night to say that the first thing Angus had asked him was how he had ended up at the hospital, and the second was who was looking after Rascal. Alister had assured the Captain that all was well, and volunteered to go over each day and check up on Rascal.

In fact, Alister thought the girls should go over with him one day soon so he could bring the *Lady Mary* back to town and have it waiting for Angus when he got out of hospital. And Angus had also asked Alister to "relay my gratitude to the young ladies for saving my life."

In the meantime, neither Emmie nor Angela had told a soul about the mysterious radio message, choosing to let everyone believe that they had sent it.

"Quite frankly," Angela had said the night before, "it's too much for my brain to figure out, so forget trying to explain it to everyone else."

But now, in the quiet of Emmie's kitchen, with no one else at home, the debate was rekindled.

"Then how did Alister get that message? We didn't even know that 'mayday' was the distress call for marine radio," said Angela.

"I don't know. I can't figure it out. In fact, there's a whole lot of stuff happening this summer that I can't figure out." Emmie wiped her mouth. "But I'm sure it isn't spooks. Mom says there is no such thing as a—"

"—ghost, so you don't believe in them." Angela finished the sentence for her, as she had so often before in this debate. "But how can you be so sure? Just because your mother doesn't believe in them, doesn't necessarily mean they don't exist."

"Well, they don't for me!" Emmie tried to cut off the argument, but Angela wasn't about to give up.

"You like mysteries, right? Well, think of this as a kind of riddle. Look at it this way: If you don't want to accept all this stuff as the work of a spirit, then let's tackle it as an unsolved mystery." She began to hum spooky music to make her point.

Emmie threw a strawberry hull at her. "Please don't sing!" she cried in mock anguish. "It's torture to my fragile ears."

"Oh, like I'm the one who got put in the back row of school choir for singing out of tune."

"I was just pretending I couldn't sing. Anyway, what about our mystery?" Emmie tried not to look too interested.

"Point number one," said Angela, holding up one finger. "The kitten in the attic mysteriously crawls across the floor and down the stairs when it can barely stand, let alone walk, and it somehow makes loud, thumping noises that wake us up. And I won't even mention the apparition I saw."

"You just did," groaned Emmie.

"Point number two." Angela was warming to her task. "Someone in a yellow raincoat stands on the dock to guide us to safety from the storm."

"I already explained that," said Emmie, adding quietly after a moment, "sort of."

"Number three. Someone radioes Alister that we're bringing in Angus, a good ten minutes after we've left his dock."

"Alister could have got the time wrong." Emmie was grasping at straws.

"Neither of us used the radio." Angela looked smugly at her friend.

"Maybe the boat radio was on and it picked us up." Emmie got up and cleared the bowls so Angela couldn't see her face. Her resolve about the non-existence of ghosts was beginning to waver.

Angela moved in with her final argument. "Neither of us said what Alister says he heard and—" she paused for effect—"the radio is never on when the boat is moored. Alister said so."

Emmie banged the dishes around in the sink without answering.

"So, Ms. Emmie Lou, if it wasn't a guardian angel or spirit, then what was it?" Angela folded her arms triumphantly.

Emmie turned with a dishtowel in her hands. Her face was red with embarrassment at being on the losing end of this argument.

She threw the towel at Angela to hang up. Then a thought struck her and she brightened.

"All right, one good mystery deserves another. We'll settle this! But first, we're going to need a quart of fresh strawberries." Emmie grabbed a basket from the top of the fridge, thrust it at a startled Angela, and led the way out to the garden.

Half an hour later they were setting off down the driveway and toward town. Emmie had a cloth bag, and she wouldn't tell Angela what was in it or what it was for.

Angela walked beside her, wondering what on earth the strawberries she was carrying had to do with mysteries and spirits, but she knew her friend better than to ask. If there was one thing Emmie loved the most, it was being mysterious. She could make an adventure out of going to William's for a pair of boots if she felt mischievous. So Angela tagged along for the mystery tour. After all, it was about time they got to the bottom of this.

CHAPTER 14

A Sweet Mystery

The two girls trudged along the highway to town, dust kicking up behind them and the hot sun beating down on their heads. Eventually, the road gave way to a wide gravel shoulder in front of the string of shops that defined the entrance to town. They rested briefly on the deserted patio of the café, shaking the dust from the road out of their hair, then Emmie went inside for a moment to let her mother know where she was going. In the heat of the intense noon sun, patrons preferred the cool of the inside over the warm shade of the patio umbrellas.

Emmie emerged a minute later, and the girls crossed to the other side of the road so they could walk along the shoulder of the highway, facing traffic. Even with the controlled-access highway that bypassed Mahone Bay, there was enough heavy truck and car traffic on this secondary highway that they had to be careful. They stayed on the shoulder until the sidewalk started on the opposite side.

Angela noticed that on these walks into town, even though the sidewalk started at the edge of the graveyard, Emmie never wanted to cross over until they were past it; she always crossed at the first of the three famous churches.

Soon they were at the T-junction of Main Street and the highway, where the Scaredy-Cat Convenience Mart stood on one corner. Emmie led the way inside the small shop.

She bought two cartons of cream and a bag of ice, putting the cream into her bag and swinging the ice beside her as they resumed their walk. Angela was feeling thirsty and very hot, and wishing she had thought to buy a drink at the Scaredy Cat.

As they walked along Main Street, they could see Emmie's whaler bobbing gently with the waves, tied up to a wharf piling on the side where the launch ramp ran down to the ocean. *Maybe*, thought Angela, *we're going out in the boat—but what do strawberries, cream and ice have to do with a boat trip?*

Instead, Emmie turned and crossed the street, walking up the steps of her grandmother's house. They paused for a minute to ring the bell, then let themselves into the cool dark of the front hall.

"Come on up!" called Gram's cheery voice. They mounted the stairs, and when Gram saw who her visitors were, she smiled and asked, "And to what do I owe this pleasure?"

"Just wanted to check up on Cutie, Gram." Emmie plunked the bag of ice in the sink and put her cloth bag on the kitchen table. She motioned to Angela to put the strawberries down there too.

"Well, she's catching up on her sleep on the porch. What have you got there, Emily?" Gram looked mystified.

Emmie smiled at Gram and put her finger to her lips. Then she drew out of her bag the cartons of cream and a plastic bag with something white in it. Gram looked at the assembled things for a minute, and then a big grin broke over her face.

"Oh, so that's what you want, you scamp. All right, off you go to the basement and find it while I get ready up here."

Emmie walked down the back stairs and into the basement. Angela trailed behind, now thoroughly confused. It was a dark, low-ceilinged basement, with great wooden beams running overhead and thick fieldstone walls that had a few tiny windows set into them. Emmie rummaged around, pulling out boxes of mason jars and old magazines. Angela stood by, being careful not to crack her head on the low ceiling. Finally Emmie gave a triumphant cry and dragged out a dusty wooden bucket.

"Here, hold it." She thrust the bucket into Angela's hands and dove back into the corner it came from. She emerged carrying a metal cylinder in her left hand, and a strange mechanism swinging by a crank in her right.

"Let's go," she said, leading the way back up to Gram's kitchen. She washed her finds while Angela settled on a kitchen chair to watch. Gram had heated the cream and some vanilla extract and sugar in a pot on the stove and was now chilling it all in the freezer. Then she scalded the cylinder with boiling water, dried it off, and poured the chilled mixture into it. She and Emmie cut up the strawberries, added them to the mixture, then inserted what looked like a paddle into the cylinder. Then they capped it with a lid. Emmie placed the cylinder into the bucket and clamped the crank mechanism over the top, and then she and Gram poured layers of ice and rock salt (Emmie's mysterious package, it turned out) around the cylinder until the wooden bucket was full. Gram placed the whole assembly into a wash pan on the floor and Emmie squatted beside it.

She looked up with an impish grin at Angela. "Well, can you guess?"

Angela shook her head. Emmie started to turn the crank and the cylinder revolved in the ice mixture.

"I'll give you three clues," Emmie said cheekily, mimicking Angela's speech about the three points of their mystery.

"First clue—strawberries."

Angela nodded.

"Second clue—ice." She kept turning the crank as she talked. "Third clue—*cream*." She said this with emphasis.

The light went on in Angela's head. "Strawberry ice cream?"

"Homemade, the best. Haven't you ever seen an ice cream maker before?" Emmie asked a little incredulously.

"Now, Emily," said Gram gently, seeing Angela's hurt look, "not everyone's made real ice cream, have they?"

"Is it as good as William's?" Angela asked. As far as she was concerned, that ice cream tasted far better than anything she had ever had before moving to Mahone Bay.

"Much better. Here! It's your turn to crank." Emmie relinquished the handle. "It takes a lot of turning before it becomes ice cream, but it's worth it."

Angela turned the crank obediently, but couldn't help wondering what homemade strawberry ice cream had to do with whether ghosts existed or not.

Time passed lazily in Gram's kitchen as they alternated cranking the ice cream and adding ice. Gram kept them supplied with tall glasses of icy lemonade as they chatted. The crank got harder and harder to turn, and eventually it was all they could do to move it.

"That's enough," said Gram, and she unclamped the crank mechanism, lifting the cylinder onto the counter. She pulled out the paddle—"It's called a dasher," she explained— and scraped it off into the cylinder, then put the cover back on. She slid it back into the ice in the wood pail and covered everything with several layers of old newspapers.

"It has to harden for a while," said Gram. "Shall we take our lemonade onto the porch so you can spoil Cutie and tell me what on earth you two have been up to?"

Angela still wondered what the connection between ice cream and ghosts was, but, she decided, at least Emmie's little mystery had the promise of a delicious ending.

But would her mystery end as sweetly?

CHAPTER 15

Spooks, Spirits, and Ice Cream

After the girls had finished their lemonades and chatted on about their summer, Gram went back into the kitchen.

"Well, you girls certainly are the talk of the town," she said as she re-emerged onto the porch and passed out the dishes of strawberry ice cream. Angela dipped a spoon into her bowl and tasted the most heavenly dessert she had ever experienced.

"What do you mean, Gram?" Emmie sputtered through her mouthful of ice cream.

"You think your rescue of Captain Targus wasn't noticed by most everyone around here? Why, I'd say half the town was on the wharf when they heard you were coming." Gram smiled at them, proud of the girls.

"How does news travel so fast in this town?" Emmie moaned as she licked the last spoonful from her bowl. Cutie got up from the wicker porch chair and thumped down onto the floor.

She marched over to Emmie and looked up as if to ask for something.

"She wants to lick out your bowl," said Gram. "I'm afraid I've spoiled her with a wee tad of ice cream now and then. Now Emmie, of course news travels fast here. It's a close community, so you live with most everyone knowing much of what you do or say. But if anyone is in need, everyone else knows right away and pitches in to help—they're that kind of people."

"So what's the talk about us?" Emmie asked.

"Just about exactly what you did, saving Captain Targus's life, and how lucky that you were there when he had his attack." Gram finished her dish of ice cream and put it down for the waiting cat.

There was a pause, then Emmie cleared her throat.

"Gram," she asked hesitatingly, "Is there such a thing as ghosts?"

Her question was greeted by a hearty laugh from Gram. "What a question, dear! Why, here we are in the middle of the most spirit-populated part of Nova Scotia, and you ask if ghosts exist. My goodness, what do they teach in school these days?"

"You mean the South Shore is full of ghosts?"

Angela sat up, excited.

"Lordy, child, there are books and collections of ghost stories from all around here. This is one of the oldest settled parts of Nova Scotia and ghosts are just about everywhere."

"But are they real, or are those just silly stories?" Emmie blurted out, but then caught the hurt look on her Gram's face. "I mean, Mom says there's no such thing as ghosts."

Another hoot of laughter from Gram caught both girls by surprise. "Your mother says what?"

Emmie felt her face redden and her voice get very small. "She says there's no such thing."

"Well, if that doesn't beat all; my daughter doesn't believe in ghosts. Let me tell you something Emily, but you mustn't tell your mother. When she was a little girl, your mother was the most firm believer in the supernatural I have ever seen. She heard angels singing and saw fairies dance in the moonlight, and there was a time when she wouldn't sleep in her room because she said she had seen a ghost there."

She paused and took a sip of lemonade. Angela looked over at Emmie, who was sitting with her glass halfway to her lips, frozen in astonishment.

"Why she is so insistent that spooks and spirits are made up, I really don't know," continued Gram. "Maybe she didn't want you to be getting nightmares."

Angela set down her glass and asked Gram with some trepidation, "Have you ever seen a ghost?"

"Have I seen one?" Gram smiled. "Well, when I was little, probably eight or nine years old, we visited Annapolis Royal and the birthplace of Evangeline—you remember the legend?"

"Wasn't she the Acadian girl in that poem about the deportation? When all the Acadians had to leave Nova Scotia?" Angela asked.

"Yes, she was," Gram replied. "And she was separated from her lover, who was forced out on a ship and sent to sea. The devastation of losing the love of her life hurt Evangeline deeply, and she searched everywhere until she found him, but he was on his deathbed. Many believe she's from Annapolis Royal, and that her ghost still haunts the fort. Now, when I was a girl, I was so taken with the story, and with being there, that I thought I saw her ghost one evening as we were leaving the fort to start for home. My parents didn't pooh-pooh it, but they didn't encourage it either. Lots of people think they see her in the mist, and maybe they do, I don't know." Gram paused as if she were going back in her mind to that time.

"Oh yes," she continued, "there was also the time I saw a light in the woods."

"What light?" both girls said at once.

"Oh, I was walking home late one evening and I was starting up the hill to the farm. We had property down Indian Road then, and as I walked through the part of our lane where the trees grew thick overhead, I saw a bright light coming out of the woods alongside the road. At first I thought it was my Papa coming with a lantern to guide me home, but it was too bright for a kerosene lamp and it moved too fast for a person walking. I was just beginning to get scared when it turned and whooshed back into the bush and went out. I never did find out what it was, but I know no one was out of our house that night and we were miles from the next farm. It was strange, all right." She paused again, thinking. "Now, why are you two suddenly so interested in ghosts?"

Angela looked at Emmie to see if it was okay to tell, and to her surprise, Emmie nodded her assent.

"It's like this," said Angela, and she explained the three strange happenings they had experienced this summer, ending with the mysterious radio message.

"But Gram," Emmie said, looking worried, "you won't go and spread this all over town, will you?"

"Of course not, my dear. Now that's one strange thing here. Everyone talks about everything, but you never hear anyone admit in public they've seen a ghost. They might tell you in private, but that's where it stays. Still, that doesn't mean they don't exist, does it?"

"Do you really think we have a…ghost friend?" Emmie said the "friend" part very slowly.

Gram mused for a minute, then replied. "Well, I wouldn't discount it. Those are things that are hard to explain any other way, and Angela even thinks she saw an apparition. I'd say that at the very least you two have someone watching over you. And I don't think it's wise to doubt his or her existence."

"We're pretty sure it's a girl or a woman," Angela said. "Don't you think so, Emmie?" Emmie still looked unsure, and was slow to answer. "I guess I have to admit that I can't really explain what happened, and the radio thing especially has me wondering. But if—and I'm not saying I believe this—if it *is* a helpful ghost, who could it be?"

"More like, who was she when she was alive?" said Gram. Then she had a sudden thought. "With all this talk about ghosts, I nearly forgot that you girls are in the paper." She jumped up and fetched the issue of the *Time n' Tide* that had been delivered that morning.

Angela and Emmie were astonished to see the headline "Local Girls Heroes!" splashed across the front page. Then they groaned to see that Mr. Woodward had used their school yearbook pictures in the article that ran underneath.

"Oh no, that's such a horrible picture of me," Emmie gasped as she grabbed the paper. Angela looked over her shoulder as they read.

> Late yesterday afternoon, two local school girls, Emily Louise Seegal and Angela Marie Black, were hailed as heroes after their daring rescue of an unconscious man from his island home.
>
> Captain Angus Targus was found in a coma on his boat moored on Mason's Island by the two young ladies…

"Oh, I'm so embarrassed. I can't believe Mr. Woodward wrote this!" Emmie cried, throwing down the paper. "Now every boy in school will be calling me 'Emily Louise.'"

Angela picked up the paper. "'Mason's Island,'" she read out loud. "Why's it called that, Mrs. Wilder?"

"It was in the Mason family for generations, so I guess it just came to be called that. At least, it was in the family until young Paul Mason lost it in a card game, so they say. It was abandoned for years until this Captain Targus bought it and moved there with his wife. They seemed like a nice couple, though I never met them formally. Then I heard that she died, and that he continued to live there all alone."

At that, the girls filled in Gram on their friendship with Angus and the story of how he adopted Cutie's brother. By now it was getting on in the afternoon, and they reluctantly gathered up the dishes and glasses and headed back into the kitchen.

Gram looked at the clock ticking on the kitchen wall. "Your mother should be here soon—her shift is over, and I gather you told her where you were?"

As if in answer, a car horn tooted below.

"Here," said Gram, thrusting the cold cylinder of ice cream into a surprised Angela's hands. "You take the rest to your family." She took off her apron. "I'll go down with you and have a word with your mother, Emily, but," she looked at the both of them, "I promise I won't say a thing about your ghost."

Emmie breathed a sigh of relief as they started down the stairs to the waiting car. As they sat in the back seat of the car while Gram talked to Emmie's mother, Angela looked at the cylinder of ice cream in her lap and thought, *One mystery solved.* But she was still puzzled—who was their friendly ghost? She sighed. *Oh well, maybe some things are never meant to be explained.*

CHAPTER 16

Cats and Clues

"You throw like a girl," Emmie shouted as she caught the ball and tossed it back to Angela. Angela deftly caught it in her baseball glove and returned it. "So do you. Maybe that's because we ARE GIRLS!"

They both laughed and stopped playing to catch their breath. It was several days later, and the girls were enjoying the last few weeks of summer vacation, throwing an old baseball back and forth on Angela's front lawn after feeding Spook.

"You catch real well, though," gasped Emmie as she sank down on the lawn to rest.

"My brother taught me," said Angela, joining her on the cool green of her lawn.

"Wish I had a brother to teach me," Emmie said with a touch of sadness.

"Well, Matt's more like a sometimes brother."

"What do you mean, sometimes?"

"He's in Ottawa at Algonquin College most

of the winter, and he only comes home for Thanksgiving, Christmas, and Easter break. And all summer he's off clearing brush with the road crew or out with his girlfriend."

"Is that the girl I saw him with last week?"

Angela laughed. "There wouldn't be any other." She got up and stretched. It was a beautiful sunny morning and all was right in the world. Captain Targus had returned to his island in good health, first stopping by to tell their parents how grateful he was for the two young women saving his life, and assuring them that he had his diabetes well under control now. Rascal, Spook, and Cutie were all growing as fast as the timothy grass alongside the road, and there were still three glorious weeks of vacation left. There was only one question mark in the whole summer that hung over the girls—who or what was their spirit friend?

Emmie had finally conceded that something supernatural had guided them in their adventures, though she still couldn't bring herself to call it (or her, as they had decided) a ghost. So for now, it was a guardian spirit.

But who was it? The question kept surfacing over and over again when the girls were alone and talking. With the exception of Emmie's Gram, no one knew about the strange happenings, and both Angela and Emmie felt it was much better left that way.

After they had put the ball and gloves away, and raided the fridge for a cool drink, they wandered up the path through the Enchanted Forest to Emmie's farmhouse. And, as was often the case, they soon found themselves sprawled out on the floor in Emmie's room, reading magazines and talking.

"Do you think we'll be in the same class this fall?" wondered Angela.

"I'm nearly a hundred per cent sure," replied Emmie from deep in her magazine. She straightened herself up and put it aside. "Mr. Woodward left a copy of the grade seven class list on his desk one day and I got a peek at it. Unless they make any changes, we're in the same class, along with Olivia and that awful Jeffrey. If he bugs me this year I'm gonna pop him one."

They both laughed at the thought, since poor Jeffrey was about half a foot shorter than Emmie and just about everyone else in the class.

"Ugh." Angela wrinkled up her face. "Why did I even think of school? It's far too early to even dream of such an awful fate. Let's talk about something nicer."

"Yeah, like who our spirit friend is." Emmie hopped up on her bed and sat back against the pillow. "This is a total mystery, and it's really bugging me. I can't figure it out."

"We just don't have enough clues," Angela said, and then thought for a moment. "The first time it happened was in this house, but the other times were at our dock and at the island. So it can't be a spirit tied to a location like some of them are."

"It might be a female 'cause of what you think you saw," Emmie added.

"I *know* I saw it," Angela broke in firmly. "And Alister thought it was one of us on the radio, so it had to be a female voice."

"Right." Emmie thought deeply. "I'm not so sure that place doesn't have something to do with it. It happened at my house, and at our common dock."

"Yeah, but what about the island?" Angela puzzled the problem. "Maybe it goes where we go."

"Or it's connected with us and all three places." Emmie was still following her own line of reasoning.

"Your Gram said that Mason's Island was in the Mason family for ages."

"That's a pretty common name around here. Could be any number of families. And what do the Masons have to do with you or me?" Emmie got up and stretched.

Angela got to her feet. "I don't think I could have much to do with it. Remember, I'm 'from away.'"

"Maybe you brought it with you from Ottawa," Emmie teased, ducking the comic book Angela threw at her head in response. Just then there was a great crash from the spare bedroom and both girls jumped.

"What was that?" Emmie said. They rushed into the room, a study for Emmie's father when he was home, and found a bookshelf hanging from one hook and a pile of books all over the desk underneath it.

"Oh, that bad Bootsie!" exclaimed Emmie. "She's always climbing up on things and knocking them down." She climbed on a chair to re-hang the shelf, while Angela picked up the books.

Suddenly Angela stopped. "Look at this, Emmie," she said excitedly. She was holding a large, old, leather-bound book.

"What is it?" Emmie got down from the chair and moved closer.

"It's an old family Bible, and look at the inside cover." Angela opened it to show Emmie. "It's got your family tree written on it."

They both peered at the fine pen markings, in different inks from over the years, that showed who was married to whom, and which children came from where. "I never knew about that," said Emmie. "I guess Mom and Dad didn't think it was important. Look, there they are at the bottom, and that's Mom's handwriting that wrote me in below."

"It looks like it's from your mother's family." Angela traced the lines with her fingers. "See, here's your Gram…" They both stared in surprise. "Mason?"

"Gram's name was Mason before she married?" Emmie was astonished. "I never knew that."

"You didn't?" Angela was equally astonished. "I mean, isn't that kind of important?"

"Not really, not to me. Maybe it's 'cause I'm adopted, though that's not really any excuse. I guess my family's not all that interested in that sort of thing. Mom probably only kept the Bible out of sentimental value."

"Do you think…" Angela let the rest of the question hang.

"Maybe." Emmie thought for a moment. "Like I said, there's a lot of Masons around. But even if she were related to the island Masons, what does that tell us about our gho—" She caught herself. "I mean, spirit?"

Angela ignored the slip of the tongue. "It might tie you to the island, and that might give us a clue as to who she is."

They placed the Bible back on the shelf and went downstairs. Bootsie was scratching at the screen door, asking to be let in. The girls opened it for her and went out into the yard. They crossed over into the barn to check whether the hens had laid any eggs. Halfway through the nests, Angela had a sudden thought.

"Hey! What did Angus say about the island?" Her voice came out louder than she meant it to.

"Angela! I nearly dropped an egg. Don't shout like that, it scares the hens. I don't remember. Wait, I do remember. He said it used to belong to his wife's family."

"Do you think she was a Mason?" Angela laid her eggs carefully in the basket as she said this.

"Could be. So what?" Emmie looked under the last hen. Then she straightened up. "Wait a second, you mean they could be related?"

Angela just grinned in response.

"But Gram said she never even met her." Emmie picked up the basket as they headed back into the kitchen. Bootsie ran back out when they opened the screen door.

"Could be a distant relation." Angela washed her hands and dried them. "Now, who could tell us that?"

"Someone who knows everybody in this town?" Emmie said absently as she washed up too.

Then they both looked at each other, and said together, "Eleanor!"

As they locked up and set off for the walk into town, something was still bothering Angela, but she couldn't put her finger on it. Where was Bootsie when the books were knocked down? Shaking her head, Angela followed Emmie down the lane and into town.

CHAPTER 17

Endings

"Well now, there's the Settlement Masons and the Sedgwick-Masons—no, they're from Newfoundland so they don't count. And there's your Gram's family; there's just her and her brother in Dartmouth. Just a minute while I get Mr. Wagner's soup," Eleanor said, walking away to serve another customer.

When she returned she continued, "Maybe if youse would tell me why you're so interested in Masons, then I could narrow it down." She folded her arms across her chest and waited.

Angela took a deep breath. "It's like this, Eleanor." She was delaying, trying to choose her words carefully—anything she said could and probably would go around Mahone Bay like a brush fire. Emmie looked at her anxiously. Angela continued. "We were researching Emmie's genealogy and wondered which Masons she was related to." Angela was glad she remembered the genealogy thing from school. And they *were* researching, anyway.

"I'm surprised your grandma hasn't filled you in on her family—but then, she's actually got two families," Eleanor replied.

"What?" asked Emmie, confused.

"Oh, wait now, let me get a napkin for Mrs. Alison." Eleanor bustled off again.

"Two families?" asked Emmie. "Someone remarried I guess."

"That's right," said Eleanor, coming around to their side of the counter. "Your grandma's father remarried after his first wife died young. Your grandma was the child of his second marriage."

"Were there any children from the first?" Emmie grasped at the significance of this turn of events. Now she understood the notation beside Gram's father's entry in the Bible—'r.m.,' for remarried.

"Hmm, that's a hard one to say. He was from Overbrooke and she was from Mahone Bay, but they settled here. Let me see." She paused and tilted her head back, thinking. A customer called her name.

"Just a minute, I'm thinking—you should try it, Hank," she called to him. Then to the girls, "Yes, there was a son, she had him real young and he went off to sea after his mom died. Don't think he ever came back." She went to serve the customer that had called her.

"So Gram has, or had, a half-brother she never knew." Emmie was getting excited at the information they were uncovering. "But where does that leave us with our friend?" She spoke in a low voice, trying not to encourage any eavesdroppers.

"I'm not sure yet," said Angela, "but somehow I have a feeling that this is all connected."

"Are you two gonna eat anything or just ask me questions all day?" Eleanor stood in front of them again, her order pad out and a mock serious look on her face. The girls knew she was joking, because she never wrote an order down, and never got an order wrong.

"Two colas and two ice creams, please," asked Emmie. They knew Eleanor would remember their favourite flavours.

"Here you are." Eleanor plunked down two spoons and two dishes—one of chocolate ice cream for Emmie, and one of vanilla with butterscotch oozing all over for Angela. She looked around to see if any other customers needed her, and seeing that they didn't, she sat down for a moment on a stool behind the counter.

"Eleanor," Angela asked between mouthfuls. "Do you know anything about Angus's family?"

"Now, sweetie, he's newly come here, so to speak. But I recollect him sayin' his wife's family once owned the island he's on."

"Would that make her a Mason?" Angela was putting pieces of the puzzle together.

"Why, I suppose it could," Eleanor looked at them quizzically. "Yes, since it's Mason's Island she must have been a Mason or a close relative to one. I'm tryin' to recollect who last were on that island."

"Gram says it was lost in a card game," Emmie chimed in.

"I don't recollect that story. Say, why don't you go over to the museum? They got lots of family histories there." Eleanor stood to help another customer.

The girls excitedly finished their snack and raced along Main Street to the museum. It was a small frame building that had once been a shipbuilder's office, and was now filled with antiques, memorabilia, and pictures of the grand days of sailing ships and fishing fleets. They were greeted by a white-haired woman at the front desk.

"Please, do you have any Mason family histories?" panted Emmie.

"Land sakes, child, slow down, nothing's going to go away too fast here." The woman got up from her desk and led them to a small sitting room lined with bookcases, with a couple of chairs and a table in one corner. "Let me see, Mader, Mareson, Mason—here it is."

She pulled out three books and read from the covers. "*The Masons of Lunenburg County* by A. Wenzil, *My Family Story* by Aberdeen Mason, as told to the Settlers Club Secretary, 1935, and *A Mason Family Tree*, compiled by Peter Mason." She put them on the table and returned to her front desk.

The two girls settled down at the table and began to leaf through the books. In *The Masons of Lunenburg County*, Emmie found documentation of her family going back to her Gram's father Albert Mason, and a reference to his first wife Anabelle, but there was no mention of children from that marriage. *My Family Story* turned out to be about another branch of the Mason family. The afternoon wore on and the search was getting frustrating. Angela ploughed through *A Mason Family*

Tree for almost an hour without success. Emmie closed her book and leaned back in the chair.

"It's hopeless," she sighed. "Most of these histories are full of old-timer's stories and recollections, and there are big gaps in the facts."

"Isn't that what Mr. Barlow said in history class, though?" Angela looked up from her book and continued. "He said history is never clean and clear. There are always different versions of events and you have to research all the relevant data and then reconstruct what seems to be the best version." She turned the page.

"Hey, here's something." Angela pointed to a chart on the page. Emmie bent over to look. "It's a family tree diagram of Masons from this part of Nova Scotia. Look, there're the Masons from that other book," said Angela, "And over here are the ones Eleanor talked about. I guess they're called the Settlement Masons because they came from Upper Settlement. What did she say about your great-grandfather?"

"That he came from Overbrooke. It's a little hamlet about twenty minutes from here." Emmie reached over and looked at the diagram. "No Overbrooke Masons there. What does the text say?"

Angela scanned the page beside the diagram. "Nothing here. Wait." She turned the page and ran her finger down it. "Here it is," she cried triumphantly, making several visitors in the museum turn and look.

"What does it say?" Emmie craned her neck to read the faded print in the book.

"'Albert Mason was the only member of the Mason clan to settle in Overbrooke. His son, Albert Jr., married a young local woman, Angeline Langile, who bore him one son and died shortly afterward. Albert raised Paul Mason himself for a number of years...'" she turned and looked at Emmie. "Didn't your Gram mention a Paul Mason?"

Emmie shook her head. "I don't remember, go on." she said eagerly.

"'...for a number of years, living for a time on an island east of the bay, until the boy ran off one day and, so it is said, went to sea, never to come home again.'"

"That's sad; first his wife dies and then his boy runs away." Emmie's voice shook slightly.

"Hold on, there's more." Angela continued to read. "'The father was distraught that his stern discipline caused the son to flee, but was too proud to admit it, and never spoke about the boy again, even after he remarried and moved to Mahone Bay. It's rumoured that the boy eventually landed in Prince Edward Island and married a Bourgogne, or so some relatives tell, but they never dared to say anything about him to the father."

"Is there anything more?" Emmie's eyes shone with hope.

Angela read ahead silently. "No, that's it. It goes on about other Masons on the South Shore." She closed the book and gathered up the other two books to put them back on the shelf. As she got up a folded sheet of paper fluttered out from one of the books. Emmie bent down to pick it up.

"This must have come from the family tree book," she said, looking at it. "See, there's another one of those drawings. It looks like someone else has been doing research here." Then her jaw dropped and she gave a gasp.

Angela looked at her, startled. "What's wrong?"

Emmie's voice croaked as she pointed, "Here's our answer—look!"

She laid the sheet carefully out on the table. The pencil lines were clear against the page. At the top was Albert Mason, connected on the left to his first wife and on the right to his second wife. On the right, below that, were Gram and her brother—Emmie's great-uncle.

But what had stopped Emmie in her tracks was the line down the left side. There were Paul Mason and his wife, Amilee Bourgogne, and below that it read, "Mary Amilee Mason, b.1938, Borden, PEI."

"That's it!" cried Angela. "Now I remember. Paul was the one your Gram said lost the island in a card game. Maybe that's why he ran away, and why his father was so angry. Where is Borden?"

"Borden's where the ferries landed on PEI, where the bridge is now," Emmie said, then, despite herself, yelled, "FERRIES!"

They looked at each other and then back at the sheet of precious paper. "Mary," Angela said. "The Captain's wife was Mary, wasn't she?"

"Sure, he named his boat after her—the *Lady Mary.*" Emmie was very excited. "And he could have met her when he sailed the ferries to and from Borden."

"And when they came out here she bought back the family island, Mason's Island. It all fits. Angus is related to you by marriage." Angela said.

"So he is. Wow." Emmie gently folded the piece of paper, slipped in into *A Mason Family Tree*, and put the book back on the shelf. She paused thoughtfully. "I wonder who drew that chart."

"Someone adding to that gap in the history? Obviously whoever it was knew about the island and its story. Maybe it was our guardian angel." Angela laughed nervously, then looked at her watch. "We'd better get going before our parents start worrying."

They left the darkness of the museum, blinking at the bright sun outside, and nearly ran straight into Emmie's mother.

"Why, there you are," she cried. "Eleanor said you were in town. I have some great news."

"And we have some for you too," said Emmie. "What's yours, Mom?"

"I just picked up the mail from the post office, and your dad sent a letter saying he'll be landing in Halifax on Tuesday next and staying home for the rest of the summer." She grinned.

"YEAH!" Emmie jumped and danced around. "Dad's coming home, Dad's coming home!" Several passersby looked at her strangely, but she didn't care.

"Come walk with me back to the car and I'll give you a lift as far as the café," said her mother. "Now, what's your news?"

Angela and Emmie told her excitedly about their research and the conclusion that Angus was their relative.

"Well, I must admit," said Emmie's mother as they climbed into the car and started off, "it does make sense, and I do recollect hearing bits and pieces like that from my uncle. It would be nice, I'm sure, for Angus to find he has family here; he seems like such a gentleman, but a bit lonely." She parked the car at the café and they all tumbled out. "Now, I'm working this evening, so you girls will have to fend for yourselves for dinner." She gathered up her baking and started toward the door. "Oh, I nearly forgot, Angus called this afternoon, so you can call him back and tell him what you've found, and see if he agrees with your conclusions."

"Call him, Mom?" Emmie sounded confused.

"Yes, he got a cell phone today. Said his scare in the hospital made him realize he'd better enter the twentieth century. With a cell phone he doesn't need to have a line strung to the island, and he can carry it with him wherever he goes. Then he said something funny about a guardian angel watching over him." With that she turned and walked into the café.

Angela and Emmie stood on the patio in the late afternoon sun. Neither of them said a word. Somewhere over the bay a gull cried, and a gentle gust of a breeze ruffled the girls' hair. They could hear the distant roar of a large truck out of sight, furiously gearing down the steep main road that levelled out just in front of the café.

Silently, they walked across the deserted patio toward the steps leading down to the road's shoulder. A sudden breeze rustled the rushes at the water's edge, and just then Angela thought she heard someone whispering in her ear. She stopped at the top of the steps and turned to look at Emmie, who had halted beside her. Emmie, too, looked like she was listening to something, and she had a faraway look in her eyes.

The truck burst into view, still going too fast, and one tire slipped onto the gravel shoulder at the edge of the road. As the driver jerked his truck back onto the blacktop, a large wooden crate snapped its lashings, whipped off the truck's open bed, and crashed into a thousand pieces on the shoulder—right at the bottom of the steps. The driver, unaware of what had just happened, roared off down the highway.

Emmie looked at Angela, her face suddenly pale. "Holy mackerel, did you see that?!"

Angela nodded, numbed. "If we hadn't stopped, we would…" she cleared her throat. "We would have been squished by that crate."

"Like two bugs." Emmie paused, letting it sink in. "I thought I heard something, and I stopped to see who was talking."

"Me too," said Angela, looking at Emmie in amazement. Then she looked behind them. The patio was still empty.

Angela linked her arm with her friend's. "I think we've got a guardian angel watching over us, too," she said.

Emmie laughed, but she didn't argue as they set off together down the road.